Sunset Park Latin King

To order additional copies, please contact us.
BookSurge, LLC
www.booksurge.com
1-866-308-6235
orders@booksurge.com

Sunset Park Latin King

Brandon Cory

2005

Sunset Park Latin King

ABOUT THE AUTHOR Brandon Cory is an ex-gang member who is using his experiences and past mistakes as a way of helping many young kids from getting involved in the gangs of New York. He has worked as a Gang Counselor for G.M.A (Gang Member Alternative. He has also appeared as a guest speaker at several seminars to speak about his past experiences within the Gangs of New York.

Short Summary From the time his father was dragged away by New York City Police Officers up to the day he walks out of prison, King Macho lives his life day by day wondering when will all the suffering he has endured end. Growing up in the hood called Sunset Park. King Macho joins a notorious gang called the Latin Kings as a way of protecting one of his younger brothers. King Macho has no idea what he has gotten himself into. Will he be able to get out of this gang in time to live a normal life or will it be to late.

Acknowledgements I would like to acknowledge those that have been very supportive: Score, Pinky, Tiny , Richie, Knuckles, Kurlz, Katie, Pun, Rick , Black, Gordo, Midas, Bebo, Electric, Roman, Allyssa , Rob, Justine, Mecca, Mellow, Ozzie, Marcus, Jesus, Ray, Solomon, Flames, Serne, Phat, Jeffrey, Pep, Boomer, Fuego, Tenaza and Ninja.Smooth.

For his input and professional expertise, I would like to thank Louis Savelli. "You're the man Good lookin!"

For being there when no one else was—My Moms, My pops, my brothers and the rest of my family.

To My brother Joe, Hurry up and make it back from Iraq safe.

Above all, I would like to thank my children that I love so very much.

Oh yes, one more thing, *No babe I didn't forget you, I love you so much, I miss that chicken cutlet , corn and mash potatoes!*

This Book Is Dedicated To Steven French "Que" And Jose Torres "Indio"

I

Where to begin, how to begin, and when will it all end? Questions that must be asked as well as answered. I love my life, I love myself, I love my kids, I love my girl, I love my freedom. Sucks because the truth is that I love it all and I sometimes hate it all, I feel alone, I feel lost, better yet I feel scared, I'm scared of who I am and what I can turn into. I want to be happy but I don't know how. If god is really there then please help me lord, help me be that person that is hidden in me. I know I can be a man with a normal life. So then why aren't I Lord. Why can't I be happy, why can't I enjoy what I have instead of hating what I don't. I'm tired of crying. I'm tired of being alone. It's funny because how can I be alone when I have brothers that love me, I have friends, I have parents, I have this, and I have that. Well the truth is that I have nothing, no one, I am alone, alone in a world where everyone acts as if they want to help you, love you, be there for you, well then my question is where were those people when I needed them most, yeah they might try to be there now, but god only you Know how I feel and what I've been through in my life, only you know how deep the scars are in my heart, in my mind, in my soul. I want to live so bad, I want joy so bad, and at other times I just want to die, die for all I have suffered, for all I know I will always suffer. What is there that I have not seen? The streets have always been there for me to explore for me to let out my frustration, my anger. The streets are my escape also my way to hell. Most of what I go through at this point in my life I can only blame myself so I've `been told, therefore I take full responsibility for, but then how about before I became this man that I so called am.How about when my mother was to busy being a mother to everyone else but her own kids? How about when she dedicated herself more to doing brujeria (Spanish for voodoo)?

MY MOTHER *"Come on Junito we have to go see my other family"* She would take me with her all the way to the South Bronx so that she can be in the basement with about 14 women and men doing their voodoo. I would sit there watching them saying all kinds of prayers. At times, this one man would smoke a cigar and blow the smoke in peoples face as part of this voodoo ritual. I hated being there. I hated the fact that my mother would travel what seemed like across the world just to do this voodoo shit. Why couldn't she be into me the way she was into this brujeria garbage? Why couldn't she be my mom the way I needed her to be. Oh, I forgot I was never really hers; I was part of a package deal. She fell in love with my father so I was part of a four people package except that she only got two out of the four people package; she got my father and me. My older brother and my older sister stood with my biological mother. So here I am, part of a package deal that went raw after maybe a couple of years. As a small child, I can say I saw it all, I saw my father come home drunk and punch my mother in the face. Other nights he was just high on who knows what. I did not understand what was happening, all I ever really knew was that everyday for months and months I would see all sorts of fighting. I would cry for hours when my father would walk out that door, cause I knew daddy would probably not come back, and when he did come back he would somehow try to make it up to me by giving me a couple of 1 dollar bills as if that would make up for the times I didn't have with him. In a way it did because I did not know no better till I got a little older but by then I deeply feel it was too late. The one thing that has always stood on my mind and I swear I know I will never forget it. One day when one day my parents were fighting and it got to where my mothers face was so swollen with lumps and cuts, sort of like the way the elephant mans face looks when you lift the bag off his head and even he looked a lot better then what my moms did. I tell you this much, I can still see it when I close my eyes. Nevertheless, the truth is that, that is not what stays on my mind the most. What does is when I hear my father screaming in the hallway and as I open the door to look down the stairs I see about six men in light blue shirts with dark blue pants beating my father up, dragging him down the stairs. I remember him throwing punches and kicking like a wild man, I remember me screaming "Papi ven aqui, core" ("daddy come here, run") as the police dragged my daddy away. My mother pulling me by my hair

MY MOTHER "Junito, te voy a meter una pela" slamming me against the wall, smacking me full force. I cried so much, so hard, not because I was being hit, not because when she brought me in the house she whipped me with the extension cord. I cried because I wanted my dad. I wanted to go with him; I wanted him home with me. But he was gone. And I swear that my mother took every opportunity she got to beat the life out of me. For some reason every time she would hit me with the belt, shoe, extension, bat, whatever she got her hands on, I swore she was seeing my father when she was hitting me. Still I loved her. She was my mom, why wouldn't I love her. Sometimes I would find little signs of her doing that voodoo stuff again. I would go into the freezer and see a cup of water with a picture of my father torn in little pieces. One day I saw her write his name on white paper and set it in a glass bowl that contained a black substance and some sort of green leaf. She then set the contents in the bowl on fire. She notices me looking in on her as she did

3

this. When she was done with her little voodoo performance she quickly went at me with the belt for being nosy. Once again I felt like I had to suffer for whatever suffering my dad had put her through. Don't get me wrong, she fed me. She kept me clean, she made sure I had a roof over my head but, when she would think about my father she would take out her anger on me and deep in my heart I knew it. I loved her, I loved her so much, I would have done anything for her, still probably would till this day but I ask myself what did I do, why me? To think I still didn't know that mommy wasn't really my mommy. There were times when my father would visit us and give us money or if not he would take us to Coney Island but when he would bring us back, Oh my god, did my father hear it from my moms! She would pick up anything she could get her hands on and throw it at him. Pots, pan, statues, shoes, knives and forks, I mean anything she found she threw at him. He would sometimes just walk away and for some reason him not fighting back when she would do this, it would get her even more pissed off. She would take the money away from us that he had given us and wait till she saw him out the window. She would yell obscenities at him and throw the money back at him out the window. This lasted for about a year after moms kicked him out, then it just didn't happen at all. He just stopped coming, stopped calling, and stopped visiting. I recall so many nights looking out the window. Watching the cars drive by. I recall my father having a red Chevy Nova, and every time I saw a red Nova zoom by, I would run to the door and stand there waiting to here the bell ring, thinking he was coming to get us, but he never came. I didn't see my dad for years that felt like a lifetime. I missed him so much. I missed the days he would bring me to the gym to teach me how to box. Me being so little, so young, I would get scared of the other boys in the gym. I was about six years old but heavyset. Therefore I had to box with boys that were about 8 or 9 years of age because we were all in the same weight class. I recall one day me being in the ring and seeing this boy bouncing up and down smacking his gloves as if he were already a professional fighter. My first reaction was to jump out the ring. I look back now and I laugh so hard at how funny I must have looked. I run to my father and tell him I didn't want to fight and that I was scared.

MY FATHER " Don't worry Macho, I'll always be here" He held me in his arms. Those days were gone; I didn't know where he was now. I would sometimes hear my mother telling my aunts about my father being in jail. Little did she know that every time she would say that, I would run to the bottom of my bunk bed and cry. I would cry till I fell asleep. I began seeing different men come to the house, they all had something I didn't like or I would find something. Johnny or instance, this was a man that owned the neighborhood grocery store. That's the store where my moms would buy food on credit when she was broke. At times I would think that Johnny was coming over to collect the money but from the sounds I would to hear late at night. He was collecting more than just money. I disliked him. He would look sloppy and dirty. He always wore these religious beads around his neck and dark sunglasses. Even when I didn't see him come in the house I knew when he was there. The house would smell so fucking nasty. The odor this man would leave wherever he went was too horrible to bear. He didn't really come over to many times, once in a blue moon. Then there was Raul. This man had an Afro bigger than J.J., and if he would have clapped his hands out loud and scream "DYNOMITE" I would have believed it was really J.J. from the show Goodtimes. The man was horrible looking. He, I didn't see very much either, he would come into the house late at night about 1 or 2 in the morning then leave after forty minutes or so. Him I just didn't like cause he had a real Tony Montana (from Scarface) way of talking. David was maybe the only cool one I felt was okay and that's maybe cause he seemed young and something about him made him look clean. Still I didn't show him any kind of respect. The truth is that any man and everyman that came to the house would only come when they believed my younger brothers and I were sleeping. Little did they and my mother know I was always awake late at night because I was either praying that my dad would come home soon or I was praying that my mother wouldn't hit me the following morning. Either way I was praying. Don't get me wrong, pity is the last thing I look for or need. But damn she mastered the art of belting my little fat ass.

2

Things did get a little better , should I say less painful. My mother started working in a clothing factory a couple of months earlier but now she was a floor manager and she worked two shifts, day and night. I was more at ease now. By the time she came home we were all in bed. We didn't go to bed hungry. There really was not much to eat. We had to always invent something. No wrong, I always had to invent something. My youngest brother was just like myself so he would eat anything. Like for instance we would eat Corn pops cereal but with water cause there was no milk. At other times we would eat waffles and make syrup out of sugar and water. There was always something I made up to make sure we ate something. As for my second younger brother, he was more difficult to feed. He only ate specific types of food. When it came to cakes, he only ate Twinkies and Yankee doodles. Rice and beans were a no-no. Chicken, steak, pork chops, and meats in general were all no-no's. Sometimes I blamed my dad for my brother not eating, I think it was my brothers way of crying out for his father that never came back. Lucky for him because we really never had any of that real good food anyway. Whenever I would go to a friend's house they would eat rice and beans with either chicken or pork chops. In my house it's eggs and rice. The beans were only if we had them and instead of a type of meat we had eggs. It wasn't that bad anyway. I still miss those days with my younger brothers. We were always fighting with each other one day and playing with each other the next. My mothers' house is small now but back then since we were so little we saw it big enough to play hide and go—seek. At other times we would play freeze tag or army. Army was my youngest brother's favorite game, he had a thing for army *toys*. If not we'd play racing cars, that was my other brother's favorite, he had over 100 Hot wheels or Matchbox Cars. We were ok when it came to us as brothers. I loved them so much as I do now. If only they knew how much I was going through but how could they when I myself didn't know exactly what was happening. Things for us changed one day when my mother came home and she saw we had broken a statue when we were playing tag. She hit us three for about 15 minutes but once again I got the worst of it. She said it was because I was the oldest. Maybe so, who knows but at least I wasn't crying alone this time. Honestly I didn't like seeing my younger siblings get hit by the chanqleta (Spanish for sandals). Just our luck one of my uncles from my fathers' side needed a place to live for a while and guess where he was offered to stay. He was now our baby sitter. I hated him. For some reason he and my father never got along. He was really mean and nasty. There were times when he made us clean the house for hours. I recall him telling me that if I clean the bathroom real good and I do a good job, he would give me ten dollars. I scrubbed and scrubbed that bathroom. I cleaned the toilet bowl. I did the best I could. When I was done I went to the living room and asked where were my two younger bros. He told me that they were in the bedroom punished because they did not do a good job. He then went to the bathroom and examined my work. I knew I didn't do a good job but I tried. He sends me back to the living room, as I walked towards the living room he walked behind me. Sitting next to me on the sofa, I see he is unzipping his pants and taking out his penis. He asked me to touch it, I declined. He then told me to do it or he will have to punish me and hit me with the belt everyday. I stood up from the sofa and told him I don't want to.

My Uncle *"ok watch what I am going to do to your little brother".* He takes my youngest brother out of the room and begins to hit him with the belt, my younger brother not knowing why he was being hit. Screaming, crying out loud. So small, so little, I was not the one being hit and still I felt his pain. I felt so helpless so scared.

My Youngest Brother *"Sorry, sorry I'm sorry"* My baby bro cried out loud not even knowing what he was sorry for. Still my uncle hit him. He did this for about 2 minutes straight. I know two minutes is not long but two minutes getting hit with the belt feels like forever; I knew exactly what my little brother was feeling. I cried as I saw my brother pleading with my uncle to please stop. I grabbed onto my uncles leg and begged him please leave him alone. My other younger brother was still in the room to scared to come out till this very day I don't think they knew what was really happening. The following day my uncle told us we had to clean the house again and that whoever did the best job would get to go to the store with him to get Mickey D's. My younger brother had to clean our room. My second youngest had to clean my moms. As for me I had to clean the living room. While my two younger siblings were doing their choirs, my uncle told me to stop cleaning. He ordered me to follow him to the bathroom. I asked *"why"?"* Just do what I tell you and hurry up or else I'll beat the living daylights out of your baby brother" he replied. I followed him. As we entered the bathroom he closed the door, pulled down his pants exposing himself. He took my hands with his and placed it on his penis. I pulled away and this made him very mad. He smacked me on my face and told me the next one would be harder and that he is not kidding when he said he'd beat my brother again. Once again he took my hand and made me grip his penis. He told me to stroke it until he said stop. This went on for months. Finally my mother kicked him out because he was not helping with the bills. All he had done was shit, sleep and eat. I also think she noticed the marks on my little brother when my uncle used to beat him. This he did on times when I tried to say no to the things he was trying to make me do. I hated him and every night I cried and swore to god that I would get even with him. I would talk to god and ask god to please kill this man for what he was making me do. My mother would sometimes walk into the room and see me crying and at times I would want her to hold me so bad, instead she would smack me and tell me to stop crying like a little girl. She thought I was crying because I wanted to stay up late. If she only knew, if she knew how much I needed her, how much I needed my dad to protect me, how much I wanted to protect my brothers from this world that seemed to be so cruel. I would talk to myself *"Don't worry junior, you're going to be big someday and no ones going to hurt you again."* It had been a while since I saw my father. I believe it was maybe years, I was never to sure about how long it had been, I had stop counting after a couple of months. On one early morning my mother woke me up and had sent me to the store to buy some pan Italiano and huevos (Italian bread and eggs). Walking down the stairs I was already plotting on what I would steal from the store. Every time my mother would send me to the store I would always steal something I knew we needed. Whether it was milk or a can of spaghetti I always came back with something extra and I would tell my mother that Johnny had given it to me for cleaning out the garbage outside his store. Every time I did this I felt as if I was doing something good for my brothers. So here I am on my way to the store thinking maybe today I'll steal a box of cheerios, as I walk out the front door I see this strong looking man with a goatee and a pushback across the street walking my way. I sensed something about him but It hadn't hit me of what it was. He walked towards me getting closer. The closer this man came towards me, the more he looked like my father. Just before he reached the sidewalk I knew it. It was he, my dad. I ran, I ran away from him, I cried, I was scared. I don't know why.

MY FATHER *"Macho, soy yo tu papa"* (Macho it's me your father) he said. I knew, I knew it was him, I didn't know how to act, I didn't know if I should be scared of him or If I should just run to him and hug him the way I wanted to. I did the later. I held on to him for dear life. I missed him so much. I cried and cried. *"Te vas a quedal"* are you going to stay I asked. He just looked at me with tears in his eyes and told me how much he missed me and that he wrote to me so many times. He walked me to the store. As he walked I skipped. Walking into the store holding my fathers hand I think to myself I wonder how Johnny is going to feel knowing my daddy's back home. I was so proud, so happy, joy was the greatest feeling I ever felt. Like everything else in my life, the feeling didn't last to long. You see, when I asked if he was going to stay he didn't answer and it was because he knew he wasn't. Basically that was the story of my life. He had a different agenda planned for himself, I guess not I, nor anyone of my younger brothers were part of it. There I was missing my father so much and for what? In many ways he wasn't there. I had to learn many things on my own. Things that a father should have been there to teach me. The things I did growing up were things that I have no idea how the hell I got away with doing but I did them. I went from stealing meat at the Keyfood to crushing Tylenol pills and selling the powder in glassine bags as if it was cocaine.

As years past I grew in size a lot bigger than the normal kids my age. I can also say I grew balls because I was no longer scared of the changleta (sandals) or the correa (belt) my mother had used on me through out the years. Shit, she was gonna have to do better than that. I was 12 Years old now and I was the most rebellious son of a bitch there ever was. My mother didn't think about going out dancing and leaving me in the house alone with my brothers because we would turn the entire house into an amusement park. The couple of times she did go out, she would ask one of her friends from next door to baby sit us and I would always look forward to them days. My mother's friend Gladys was a wonderful person. My brothers and I loved being home with her; we were always at our best behavior whenever Gladys came around. This lady taught me so much. It began when she was watching us one Friday night and my mother went out. It was about 11:30 pm. Both my brothers are sleeping and I'm in the bathtub with one of my cousin's favorite playboy magazines. My cousin and I would collect all sorts of perverted magazines and trade with each other. On this one night I had one of my cousins best mag. It had nude pictures of one of the Charlie's Angels. I believe it was Farrah Fauset or something like that. So here I am in the bathtub choking the chicken in Farrahs name not realizing the door to the bathroom was unlocked. Gladys walked in scaring the shit out of me and shrinking my teenage prick back to shribble size. I was never so embarrassed in my entire life.

GLADYS " *I'm so sorry, I didn't realize anyone was in here"* nonchalantly saying as she closed the door. *"That's it, the sexscapade with Farrahs over"* I washed up and out the tub. As I was drying myself up Gladys knocks on the door.

GLADYS " *Are you almost done yet?"* and I answered with an annoyed tone " *yeah can you just please give me a break".*

GLADYS "I just wanted you to know I picked out your pajamas and they're on your mothers bed, ok* "This lady was really starting to become a pain in the ass. Here I am trying to bust a bubble or better yet a nut and this fucking baby sitters ruining my sexual encounter with righty. After drying off, I wrap a towel around my waste leaving the bathroom to enter my mothers' bedroom. Opening my mothers' bedroom door, the unthinkable happened. Gladys was lying on the bed totally naked.   *GLADYS* *"Come here little boy"* I couldn't move. I was stuck in place. My heart was racing. My once shribbled prick was now a swollen monster. I Just couldn't get my eyes off her body. All these crazy thoughts were running trough my head. Farrahs got nothing on my great babysitter. Is this all a dream?

GLADYS *"I said come here"* Tapping her hands on the bed signaling for me to lay next to her. *GLADYS* *"I want to teach you something but only if you swear and promise not to ever tell a soul"* No words could come out of my mouth and if they could I just didn't no what to say. I just climbed onto the bed and laid next to her with my hands on my side, my eyes staring at the ceiling. My body trembling

.*GLADYS* *"Ok, I'm going to touch you and if you want me to stop I want you to say so ok, if not then I will continue"* I just nodded my head up and down, my only way of saying yes because still I could not speak, as if my jaw was wired shut.

GLADYS *"Close your eyes to help you relax"* I looked at ladies or women before in all the magazines. I've seen dozens of naked pictures of women but never did I realize how sexy a lady could really be. I never understood women, how could I, I was young. I'm not too sure I understand them now. Gladys was gorgeous. I never noticed this beautiful thing, I always looked at her as my babysitter because that's what she was but now she was more. My eyes close, my hands to my side. I feel her touching my face with her fingers, gently, slowly. My heart racing but I'm no longer nervous, I feel relaxed and turned on. She continues to caress me slowly, but now using her tongue. Feeling the wetness of her tongue sliding around my neck, licking me, kissing me

GLADYS *"Do you want me to stop little boy, do you"*? With my eyes still closed I move my head from left to right, not realizing the word no was coming out of my mouth. She brings her face up to my lips and kisses my mouth all the while she's holding my friend that is now her friend as well. She slides her tongue in my mouth. It feels weird but good. My body feels hot. My mind feels dazed. She goes back to kissing my neck, whispering in my ear

GLADYS *"Do you want me to kiss it? Do you want me to continue?"* I didn't have to answer she new the answer her self. She knew she had me literally in the palm of her hand. I was on cloud nine. She licked my chest, working her way down to my stomach with her tongue, still lifting my testicles with one hand and jerking my now solid throbbing buddy with the other hand.

GLADYS *"If you want me to keep on you have to say you'll do anything I say. If not I'll stop right now, so tell me baby, do you have something to say Sweetie?"* Gladys was my master, I never felt this way before. I don't know what it was or how I was able to say it but I said it" I'll do anything you say, I swear, please don't stop, I like it so much please" she smiled at me as she heard me say the word. I felt pain, my penis was so hard and throbbing so much that it was beginning to hurt me but what a pleasurable pain it was. She began jerking my manhood faster and faster *"ooh you're nice and hard and I think it's time I give you your surprise little boy, imma turn you into a man".* With those words said, she guided my penis into her mouth, all the while still jerking him off with one hand and caressing my balls with the other. Licking the tip with her tongue then taking it fully in her mouth. This feeling I would not trade for the world. My body quivering, my balls tightening, my penis throbbing. I've masturbated before but this feeling was like having all the fantasies I've masturbated to, come true. The feeling was so wonderful that finally I was reaching that point. *"Oh goddddddd"* I yelled out as my penis unloaded it's cum into

Gladys mouth. This little scenario continued between Gladys and myself for about a month or two and then it just stop. It's weird because I know that she was no different than my uncle was. The truth is whether I enjoyed it or not, she sexually abused me but for some reason I didn't see it that way, I just can't explain it.

I'm a big man now, so I think! No more staying home with my two younger brothers. The streets are calling me and there was no way I wasn't going to answer. I'm going outside was all I would tell my mother, she would fight, scream and yell at me, *"Junito, you're not going anywhere"* but the truth is that I was past that. There was no holding me back now, I was bigger, stronger and I felt the need to get out of the house. The thoughts and memories, no way was I going to stay home all day. I began with just standing in front of my building for the first couple of months. That's all I knew, my block and the streets that I would take to go back and forth to school, but things were about to change. I'm 14 years old now and I'm in Dewey Junior High School. The kids were older and the girls seemed developed as for me I was a freshman but I seemed like a senior to everyone else because of my size. I loved going to school, oh no don't get me wrong, normally kids were going to school to get an education and to work on their future. Me, well I went for the free breakfast and lunch. I went for the girls, school fights and cause I had no choice but to go. The one thing that I was automatically drawn to was the bad kids in school. They were always wearing colors and clothing that had their gang names. No matter where you turned there were thugs around you. For instance in the morning I would walk to school and see older gang bangers from high schools walking their younger brothers to school and someway somehow they would end up fighting with other kids that were wearing colors from other gangs. I would stand there and watch the fighting. At 2:45pm everyday, now that was the best time to always see fights. On 41st and 4th all the thugs from every other gang would congregate, on that corner fights were normal, rumbles were the talk of the day everyday. During the day, in the school I would always have someone letting me know that their cousins or brothers wanted to know if I wanted to be part of their gang, I would always say no but deep in my heart I wanted to say yes. I mean this was Sunset Park, home of some of the toughest gangs in the city. The Dirty Ones, they were into selling drugs. The Assassinators, any extortion in the hood best believe they were getting the dough. The Familia, robberies were their specialties. The Macheteros, they were into everything and anything. The Turban Saints, The Chingalings, The Vandal-izing Crew, The Masters of Disasters, BRB, ASD, PSB. The list went on and on .The one thing that they all had in common was that they was all hardcore thugs. It was all about respect. Members of these gangs all had either tuff names or cool names. I recall hearing names like Demon, Speedy, Crazy, Spider, and Palo Viejo. Shit I always told myself I had to get myself a nick-name, For some reason Junito didn't sound to tuff.

It's boring at home, my mothers working and my grand-mother was now watching my brothers. I go to my friend's house, George and see if he wants to hang out in front of the building. So there we are standing in front of my building just listening to his boom box. We end up in the corner of my block hanging out in Cuckoo Mikes. Cuckoo Mikes was a fast food restaurant the guys on the block would hang out at. They had several arcade games Dig Dug, Pac Man, Defenders. We would hang out there and play games and look at the pretty ladies that would come in to buy chicken. On this day, Mike, the owner of the place, kicked us out cause we were harassing the customers. We then end up back outside bored, that's all we knew the block and school. The hell with it, I asked George if he wanted to take a walk to 5th Avenue to go look at the girls.

GEORGE " *Uh, my moms don't let me leave the block plus it's dark outside.*"

Myself *"The hell with this I'm out " I was on my way.*

It was windy and cold. The night seems young, actually it felt like morning. Like when you wake up at six in the morning but its dark outside. Well that's how it seemed. No there are no chickens making those annoying sounds as if they were the early morning alarm clocks waking up the neighborhood like they usually do in this Boriqua hood called Sunset Park. All you heard were people laughing, cars honking their horns, the avenue felt crowded. I could see hundreds of people walking around with all kinds of goodies in their hands. What truly stands out the most are the sparkling lights coming from every storefront. Like when you are watching T.V and you see pictures of Las Vegas and all the lights are on at night. That's what 5th avenue felt like The funny thing about walking on the avenue is that it seems as if everybody's related to everybody one way or the other. I mean, you could see my friend Carlos talking to his cousin Willie in front of the Keyfood Supermarket where his brother Joe works with his girlfriend Maria. The left bone connected to the right bone, right? Well, as for me I was just enjoying my walk and looking at the honeys. One thing that really caught my eye were the colors that dudes was wearing, some were wearing rebel hats with their names painted on the side of the hats others were wearing leather vest with their gang names on the back of the vest. Then there were others that wore black and red windbreaker pants and jackets. No matter which way you look there were gangbangers walking the streets. Every now and then you would see posters of the movie WARRIORS hanging on the light poles. Warriors was the name of the movie that was playing in the Coliseum Theater on 52nd and Fourth. I'm feeling a little tired so I stop at the Mikes Pizzeria on 49th and 5th. I buy myself a slice with some change I had found in the sofa the day before when I was looking for my pen. I had only enough to buy a slice but no drink so I asked the man for a cup of water. While I'm sitting down I notice 2 guys staring at me. They were kind of mean looking to but I just looked the other way. Obviously they were both in some kind of gang because they were both dressed exactly alike. Blue jeans and MC wallets hanging sticking out of there left pockets. They were the type of wallets that had those long chains attached to them. They also had a key chain with feathers hanging from their hips on the same left side where the left pant leg was rolled up to their knees. They both had leather bombers and they were both wearing MC boots. The truth is that right there and then I was asking my self why the hell didn't I just stay on the block with George. I was trying to eat my slice as fast a possible while at the same time not looking towards their direction but to no avail, they both came towards me and I swear to god I thought I felt my pants getting wet from me pissing on my self. But nah, it was my cup of water, I accidentally knocked it and didn't even notice. *"YO, who you be"* asked the shorter guy, I didn't answer, I couldn't cause I really didn't understand what he was asking. *" Hey punk, my peoples is talking to you "* now the taller guy is talking to me and all I can say was *"I'm sorry I didn't understand the question".* The taller guy pulled me by my jacket and dragged me to the bathroom while the shorter one kept the clerk busy. *"I asked you, your fucking name punk"* here I am in the fucking bathroom getting ready to get my ass kicked and robbed. *" My name is Junito"* that was all I could say. *" What kind of name is that, what gang you roll with"* He asked while he slapped me in the face and searched my pockets. I don't know what came over me but everything I've ever been through, all the ass whippings my mother and uncle gave me, all the pain I had inside of me, along with the anger, it all came out of me right there in that bathroom. I swung at this guy with all I had. Punching him in the face, the stomach, every where I could hit I was hitting him, that was until his partner came in and all I saw was fist after fist after boot after boot. As I lay on the ground the taller gangster looked down at me *"Look man, you're a tuff young one, to bad you're not one of us"* Then he kicked me one last time as the shorter guy laughed. " You gotta get a better name then Junito mamas boy" They left the pizzeria and I cleaned myself up. I was basically proud of myself. I stood up to those gangbangers even though I took an ass whipping. The one thing that did get to me was what they had said about my name. It was true, I needed to stop having people call me Junito I hated that name. The only person that never called me that was my father and that's cause he used to call me his macho man. Hey that's it, MACHO. For now on, I want everyone to call me as my father did. Macho was my name for now on and I will not answer to any other name.

5

THE REAL

Are we on the air? Oh OK, This is Lisa Lolita, of Street Warriors and I'm on 67.4 Fm This week we're going to talk about teens raised in the hood with only drug dealers and gang members as their role models. Today I will not be taking any calls for I have a story to tell then next week I will be accepting calls dealing with the story I have told today. This story is about a young man who was raised in the heart of Sunset Park Brooklyn. At one time he was a very happy young man just having dreams of owning his own home with a big backyard and a dog running around. He dreamed of one day having a beautiful family to share it with, but dreams were just dreams. As this young man who I will name as Macho, as he reached his middle teens he was what you can all call a good bad guy. I mean you've all met someone who you would consider a good bad guy. Well, Macho knew all the good people in his neighborhood. Tony from the pizzeria, Mike from the chicken place on the corner called Cuckoo Mikes. They would always tap Macho on the back of his head or mess his hair up while saying "You're a good kid Macho always stay that way" Macho knew all the good people and they really liked him but believe me he also knew all the bad people as well . Like for instance the drug dealers that would hang out on the corners. They would call Macho over, "Hey Macho, come here stand over there on that corner and whistle if you see the "five O" coming" He would do it once in a blue moon, seemed harmless to him. No big deal he would think". Ladies and gentlemen, I have to go to a commercial break but just for a few minutes, don't leave your seats or don't change that dial. I will continue this story in just a few minutes.

6

I'm walking around school like I'm a big willy now, since that fight I had at the pizzeria, I've blown up with props. That's all everyone is talking about in school, How Macho fought with Danny Dee and J.R. Shit, the sad thing about all of this popularity is that I didn't even know who they were, it turned out that they were leaders of a well respected gang and I someway somehow managed to give Danny Dee a black eye. Hey, more power to me. Everyone is talking to me, giving me high fives, girls are smiling and winking at me, you know that had me with my head swollen. As I'm walking through the hallways this ninth grader , stop me short on my tracks , *" Hey you , what the fuck you doing wearing that shirt?"* I'm looking at this guy like he must be confusing me with someone else. *"Do you know who I am?"* If I knew who he was, I wouldn't be looking at him like I didn't but some people just asked the stupidest questions. He was about 5'11 stocky frame, black bandana over his head and black outlaw shirt that said easy rider on it. I was wearing the exact same shirt. *" Big Man, you're wearing the same shirt I'm wearing"* My response was*" I guess I'm a biter!"* he just looked at me and we both started laughing. *"What's up my name is Nel what's yours?* I extended my hand and responded *" Macho"*. From that they forward everyday in J.H.S was a party for me. We had hooky parties every Friday in my mother's house while she was working. Nel had the hook ups with the weed and liquor, I had the hook ups with the ladies. One day Nel and I met up with about 6 girls and 5 of Nels friends. Lil Chip, Vest, Black D, Jay and Tony we went to my mothers house and they were smoking weed like there was no tomorrow. The girls we had with us were just as bad. They were getting twisted. There we were laughing up a storm, dancing and having a good time listening to Big Daddy Kane. Nel asked me if he can bring one of the girls to my brothers bed so they can do the nasty and get high some more. *"Go ahead, but don't break the bed"* Shit , I was going to try and get me some ass to , there was no way I was going to forget the moves my old baby sitter had taught me back when I was a little nigga, nah mean. There sitting on the kitchen table was Veronica. I knew she liked me but I never dared speak to her but now that I got all these props and I'm respected in the school, shit Imma hit that.

Myself "What's up V, you aight?"

VERONICA "Yeah pa, just tired, I wish I could lay down for a few but these niggas hogging up the couch, that's why I'm sitting here on this damn table" Hummm, this was a perfect opportunity for me to make my move.

MYSELF " how about if I open my moms room door and we go chill in there?" *VERONICA* "Yeah, pa that sounds proper, want me to bring the Buddha in there with us?"

MYSELF "Go ahead do you but I ain't smoking, weed ain't my high nah mean!

VERONCIA "nah pa, I don't, so what's your high then"

MYSELF " You, you goin be my high " So we get in my mom's room and she lays down while puffin on a joint. While she's smoking I'm caressing her face gently with my fingers.

MYSELF "damn ma, your skin feels smooth , ya heard"

VERONICA "That's not the only thing that's smooth Machito, go ahead, touch" spreading her legs as if letting me know she wants me to feel her. Her wish was my command. I kissed her lips while I played with her pussy, she felt smooth and wet both at the same time, the more I kissed her and rubbed her pussy the more she moaned. Remembering what Gladys had taught me, I automatically went down on her, within minutes it was heaven for Veronica. I knew she came, I think I figured out when she yelled *"Yesss"* About a dozen times then her body just went limp. Ok, I did as I was taught, I satisfied her first and now it was my turn. Veronica felt tight, everything about her was awesome, the way she kissed, her eyes, her lips, the one thing that I didn't like was the smell of weed in her mouth but that was easily forgettable once I was pounding away like a raving bull. What really sucks is when you're right in the middle of busting a nut and someone knocks on the door, fuck this, Imma finish this.

Nel *"Yo, Mach, we all out, got to go back to Dewey for when everyone comes out we there"* They left and Veronica and I put our clothes on, I walked her home and on my way back, to the house I noticed smoke coming out of my moms window. I ran up to the front of the building to see what was going on and there were about 3 fire trucks there. My moms crib was on fire. After it was all and done with, the fire marshals found it to be a short circuit but I knew better. Veronica left her fucking joint on in the room and the fucking shit burned my moms apartment. Thank god, the damage was minimal but my hooky days were over, no more hooky jams in my crib. I stopped hanging out with Nel and started concentrating on doing good in school so that I can make my graduation a gift to my moms

Junior High School for me was all fun and games but I made it, I graduated and I was on my way to high school, John Jay High School. That was one of the worst schools in Brooklyn. I was now about 16 years old. If it wasn't had I didn't get into it. I recall one cold winter, I think it must have been the winter of 1987, I'm on 5th avenue walking towards my old girlfriend Veronicas house. When who do I see, J.R the same guy I had a fight with 2 or 3 years ago. I really wasn't worried. He had nothing on me, my hand skills was to vicious for this punkass chump. From the corner of 48th and 5th I could see him on 49th and 5th walking my way , there was no way in hell I was going to cross the street or turn around. Whatever was whatever, right in between those blocks we both came face to face with each other, he seemed a lot shorter than what I could remember. He looked at me straight in the eye and pushed me. I fell to the ground but once on my feet, I hit'em with the 1 and 2, that was all she wrote. He fell to the ground, busted nose and bloody lip. I now looked at him, recalling the words he and his buddy had once said to me, I looked at him and I said *" You got to get a better name than just J.R , mamas boy".* As I turned my back to walk away, someone yelled out for me to look behind me. I turned and J.R had a butterfly knife in his hands coming towards me aiming towards my stomach, I did the only thing I could. I ran. I ran till I ran out of breath. I turned around to look and he wasn't there, I thanked god he wasn't. Right there and then I had decided that I will carry a knife myself, whether it be a butterfly knife or a butter knife, either way I was going to have one on me. I go into the chinito store called Treasure Island on 56th and 5th and I buy myself a utility knife, that's one of those knives that has everything on it, screwdriver, razor, scissors , and yes a knife. I walk down to 59th and 4th, hop on the train so that I can get home, I was too tired to walk. Here I am sitting on the train with my knife in my hand looking at all it's gadgets, I opened it and checked out its little scissors and screwdrivers. The man sitting across me stands up , stands right in front of me *" ok, when the train stops , I want you to get off the train quietly and respectfully, I am an officer and I want to see some I.D."* aww shit, I was pissed, my first instinct was to run , but to where? The train was moving. The train stops and we both get out. Once off the train, the officer slams me up against the wall, twist my arms and slaps the cuffs on me,

POLICE OFFICER *"You have the right to remain silent, anything you say can and will be used against you in the court of law"* He went on and on, and I'm just thinking to myself, this can't be happening to me. I get to central bookings, the truth is I was scared shit, but once I got to Brooklyn house, it felt like I was in sunset park all over again, 72 hours later , November 18th 1987 I see the judge and my case was dismissed. I get on the train on Atlantic Avenue and once I reached the block, it felt like I was a fucking movie star. *"Yo Macho, oh shit my nigga, how was the pins?"* asked Raycat. He was an old G from the block. But I didn't even answer, I just ran to the house to take a shower cause I stunk like central bookings.

The props for me with the younger kids in the block was happening. They all wanted to hear stories of me being locked down. I felt as if I had just finished doing a long bid. I'm not even going to front, them 3 days felt like a month. But it wasn't long before I ended up in bookings again. I didn't want to be in school, I use to cut out everyday, so not even 30 days later I'm hanging out in front of Dewey J. H. S , everybody else was there so fuck it , why couldn't I? Maybe cause I was to tall, that's why. Every fucking time I was chilling in the corner hollering at the girls, Five O would come and fuck with me, like I was the only one there. I remember it was a couple of day before Christmas and I'm chillin right on 41st and 4th and on that day Five O decided they were going to make an example out of me so that the rest of them other niggas would not come around the school no more. Damn bitch cop , locked me up for criminal trespassing . I swear I couldn't believe this shit. Twice in about a month! 12-21-87 I see the judge and I'm let go on a conditional discharge. Fuck this, no more for me , I ain't chillin by that damn school no more, I kept telling myself while in them smelling fucking pins. This time I meant it.

8

Ok fans listening, this is Lisa Lolita from street warriors and I'm here at 67.4 fm telling you all a story about a young man raise in the hood. This story is very interesting and I will be taking calls next week from fans on what they feel about this story.

So Macho begins to talk to drug dealers that he believes are just cool dudes hanging in the corner. He does them a favor here and there and that's where I left off. He began getting into minor troubles but he would brush it off. He believed in his heart he had good reasons for doing many of the things he did. He was wrong but he still was a good bad kid who would always help that one little old lady cross the street or help some old man carry his groceries. He would help Tony from the pizzeria clean up, or he would do the garbage for Mike at the chicken place, the neighbors saw him as a good kid. But those days of being good didn't last to long. He started noticing that all the people that liked him or would tap him on the head as if saying hello, they were now ignoring him and acting as if he didn't exist and all the thugs in the corner that use to hang out in that corner are now scared of Macho. They were scared of the new but worst Macho. The baddest they've ever seen him. Why? Who was this they were now seeing, he was still Macho wasn't he? No, not even close he was no longer that cute little young good bad guy everyone in the hood liked so much. Now he changed he was the man, the real tuff guy. He felt like the ruler, the master, the untouchable. Not many people felt this way and not many people ever do unless you're a god or the president and even he has his bad day, thanks to Monica. Who did Macho think he was, superman? No he thought he was a king, actually he was but not like the king of England, far from it. He was a Latin King as in the well known notorious Latin King Nation. For those that don't know, The Latin kings are considered to be one of the biggest gangs in many states including N.Y. The leader *of this gang is now serving a life sentence in a maximum federal prison. The Latin Kings had started in Collins correctional facility on Jan of 1986. By Luis Mendez Felipe also known as King Blood The Inca. He started out with just 5 members but by the mid 90's he had an estimated 15,000 members in and out of the prison system. Macho became one of those 15,000 members. He really believed that he was some tough guy . No one would even look at him the wrong way and if they did he would have about 200 Latin kings there making sure that the person would never look at macho that way again. There was even this one time when this young black kid wearing a red bandana over his head, had thrown a bottle towards machos way. In a matter of minutes Macho had gotten 50 Latin kings there with just one phone call. They found this young black kid and broke his hand so that he can never throw a bottle at a Latin King again. Sorry ladies and gentlemen, time for a commercial break. But don't touch that dial, the story gets better. Got to pay the bills or the bosses will get on me. I'll be back on the air within the next 10 minutes.*

9

Myself "*Nel, what the fuck is going on, why ya*

Yeah, the spring is here and I'm chillin, I got a job working in a shipping dept on 36th an 3rd. Loading and unloading trucks. I was making that paper. My name still ringing bells in the streets. Still popular, still respected but on the low for the last 5 years, trying to stay out of trouble. Surprisingly I haven't gotten arrested for nothing and haven't been into shit. Some might have even said I straighten out my life but between all of you reading this and me, shit I was being a smart dude. I was what my friends use to call me , a good bad guy, I was working and doing my dirt on the low, I had learned that the real bad boys weren't the ones hollering , making noise, fighting. The true bad boys were the ones being bad without anyone knowing anything about what he was doing. Shit I was working at this warehouse for 4 or 5 years straight, I was caking it! Making money legitimately and at the same time taking it illegally. Everything was going ok for me till one day, I go visit my mother at her house and to no surprise, she wasn't there so I laid down on her sofa waiting for her to get home. Instead my brother Jay came in with a swollen hand, He was telling me how he had seen some young bucks on 42nd and 5th and he had knuckled one of them down for staring at him. " *I broke the kid with the knuckle, that's how you taught me Macho*". He was proud of himself, hey so was I. He got himself something to eat and we both sat down, he began telling me the story. Not halfway into his story that the bell rang. "*Who is it?*" I'm looking down the hallway. " *Is Jay there?*"

I hear someone asked, but as he is asking I also hear other guys in the background screaming, lets kill his ass. My street smarts kicked in and my first instinct was to say no. *" Nah, he ain't home"* and I went back in. The bell rings continuously. This time I didn't answer it, I just went downstairs to see who it was. I reach out to open the front door to the building and I felt a sharp pain in the back of my head. It was this short fat dude that punched me with full force. How did I not fall, I don't know but I fought back . Eventually I rocked the kid, I grabbed him by the neck and practically carried him out the door when all of a sudden I see about 20 to 30 guys charging at me, I let go of the cat I was holding by the neck and I started swing like a wild kangaroo but my swings were no match for the 30 or 40 punches coming at me. I got hit on every single part of my body. All I saw was stars, don't get it twisted, I fought back but realistically how much damage did I really do, nada! *" Amor De Rey, okay guys stop this isn't him".* I heard someone say with a deep voice. He sounded familiar but I just couldn't connect it. " Get away from him, this isn't him" Obviously the man speaking must have been the leader of this gang. They were all dressed in black and yellow. Yellow bandanas, yellow and black beads around their necks. *" Macho, that's you?"* It was my old friend Nel from Dewey J.H.S. He came to me and shoke my hands like if I was in the mood to shake anybodies fucking hands. *"Playa, what's up with you, why you fighting with my bros?"* he stands there and asked me like if I am the one that went to their house and beating them like a pimp beats his ho. *niggas did me dirty like this for?"* I asked

NEL *"Nah, man your little bro Jay just beat up one of my bros so we got to do what we got to do"*

Myself *" fuck that ya gotta get through me first cause ain't nobody touching my bro"* I responded

NEL *"Macho, lets you and I take a walk and discuss this aight!"*

He explained that the hood is different now, most of the peoples in the hood that use to be down with a gang have either hung it up or became Netas or Kings. He spoke to me like if I knew what the hell he was talking about. I think he realized I had no idea so he continued to be more informative. He first explained that my brother got into a fight with a member of the Almighty Latin King Nation. Once again I had no idea what Latin Kings were. He continued, Latin kings are an organization build by the Latinos for the Latinos. He also explained that their goals are to uplift the Latino community, to make a difference and to show the young Latinos right from wrong. I'm still looking at him like I'm lost and still he continued. Latin kings are here to help Latinos overcome the obstacles of everyday life, to inspire the personal social and economic growth and needs of our people. Now I'm looking at him like I am understanding but the truth is , I really didn't care I was just letting him talk cause I really needed to rest and the longer he talk the longer I rested just incase I had to get my ass kicked again.

"Macho we the Latin Kings are here to preserve and to protect the entire Latino community" I just looked at him with that smart alec look, *"Nel can I ask you one simple question? Does my brother look white to you, or maybe Chinese or something, because if he does I want you to know, he's Latino, so then why you trying to kill him?"* He explained that when a person, any person, may it be Spanish, white, black, purple, it didn't matter , when they go against the Latin kings , they will have to feel the power of the Latin kings as a whole. He told me that the only way that my brother would be safe is if I would join the Latin Kings myself, that way, no one would be allowed to hurt him. The rules were, never to hurt a family member of a Latin King. I decided to become a member. Better safe than sorry, I thought.

NEL *"OK, but first let me explain to you what position I hold as a Latin King. I'm first crown.*

Nel, explained to me about the 5 leaders of a tribe or a group of Kings from a certain section. Each leader held a certain position and with each position came a certain job.

1st crown – President of the Tribe or group.

2nd crown—Vice President of the tribe or group

3rd crown—Warlord, Minister of Defense

4th crown—Treasurer

5th crown—Adviser for the above crowns.I listened and tried to remember everything he was explaining. The next day, Nel gave me The Five Points and

The Kings Prayer.

RESPECT—Respect for your brothers crown and nation and a Kings respect would show high in regards to his nation.

HONESTY—Mark by the truth, your word is your crown, your crown is your nation, a king will live and die by his words.

UNITY—The conditions of being united into a single whole, one for all and all for one, the crown symbolizes our people Latinos. ADR

KNOWLEDGE—The knowing of your lessons and prayers gained through experience and the studying of your nation

LOVE—Love is what we carry in our hearts for our brothers crown and nation.

The prayer

Almighty father king of kings we the Latin kings are 360 degrees strong in knowledge understanding and respect. I promise here on this very day and in front of the almighty father that I will be by my brothers side trough good and bad situations, I also understand that I will die for my brothers if I have to . I understand that any verbal or physical harassment towards anyone of my brothers will be considered a violation to this nation. I also understand that I would die for my brothers if I have to. I understand that any orders given to me by anyone of my superiors I am to follow these orders with no excuses whatsoever. I understand that no one forced me to be a member of the Almighty Latin king nation therefore I will be a king till the day I die. Amor De Rey.

10

Hello everyone this is Lisa Lolita with street warriors at 67.4 Fm and I'm telling you guys a story about a young man who is raised in the hood, his name is macho. So there he is standing with all these young gangbangers around him waiting for the next move. They just broke another persons arm who I was just informed was a member of the Park Slope Bloods. Do you know what Macho's state of mind could have been at that time. Well he had told me in an interview 2 years ago that he felt high, High of the power he had. Knowing that he could have hundreds of people at his command was a high that he was falling in love with. He was proud of being a Latin king. He was black and gold forever. He had once stated to me that the Latin kings had problems with many other gangs or nations like the five percenters or the crips but the one gang they had problems with the most were the bloods. They were the second toughest gang right under the Latin kings. The reason he didn't say the biggest was because the bloods were far from the biggest. You had the Netas , Zulu Nation , Los Papi chulos, but the Bloods were just the wildest and the most heartless. No one paid that much mind to the bloods in the late eighties and early nineties because the Latin Kings were just to well known. They were in the newspapers almost everyday and the news was always naming Latin king members that were getting locked up for some crime that they had committed but as Macho had told me during our last interview ,for every one Latin king that goes into the prison system , 3 are coming out. " We never die we multiply" he had said proudly .That was true for about 3 to 5 years straight but with power and numbers came blood and pain. The Latin Kings didn't fear any one of its enemies but just like Macho, the one enemy they didn't expect to get beaten by was the most dangerous one. I know you listeners are probably naming different gangs right now but just think about this, their worst enemy had guys that were cold blooded murderers , rapist

, robbers, drug dealers, thieves, everything and anything you can think of , that's what made their worst enemy so dangerous. Ladies and gentleman, as Macho once stated to me. The Latin Kings worst enemy are the Latin Kings themselves. Things for macho were getting out of hand, he began to see himself in a cell or a grave but it was to late, there was no way out. He never admitted this to any one but he began to get scared. He noticed members of the gang or nation as he called it, they were killing each other and it was going to be a matter of time before one of his own kill him. I'm sorry ladies and gentlemen but my bosses are reminding me that we have to pay the bills once again, we are going on a commercial break but we will be back here with you on 67.4fm within the next few minutes.

April 1992 – I'm still not a full Latin King but with all the props I already had on the streets before meeting the Latin Kings, I was a shoe in already, I was on probation. Meaning I already had one foot in. I'm with King Nel and we were going to the auto shop to check up on a car I was having painted. It just so happen that Jesus, that was the owner of the shop, he told me point blank that he wasn't going to paint the car unless I give him another 1000$ dollars. This really pissed me off because I had just given this man 1500$ in cash. He told me either give him a thousand more or take the car with the risk of losing the fifteen I had already given him. Now how stupid was I suppose to look standing here and letting this man jerk me around right in front of King Nel.

NEL *"Macho, what you goin do, you not goin let him get away with that right?"* Fuck, now I was put in a situation where I had to do something or look soft. " Nah, I'm good, don't worry, you know me bro, you know how I do" On May 1st of 92 I go with Nel to 19 street. Without telling him what I'm about to do, I just walk up to a burgundy Mercury Cougar and I break the windows. I then emptied a can of lighter fluid into the front seat, lit a match and we wouldn't have to wait for July to see fireworks. Nel looks at me with a shocked look on his face " *Holy Shit, come on lets go Macho,* *run"*. We ran to 29th and third. He took a cab home from there and I stood hangin out with some yayo pushers I knew from that block, see if them dealers got anything worth taking off them. Before I could even plot against one of them, two men wearing long trench coats, jump out of a four door caprice. *" Ok, Macho, you know the drill,"* They were Fire Marshals. *" Nah officers, I don't, wont you come here and show me"* Me and my big mouth, they put a beating on me and purposely tighten the cuffs so to stop the circulation on both my hands. Arrested for Arsoning in the 3rd. Central Booking here I come. This time I hit the Rikers Island because I had no one in court to pay my bail so they shipped me to the Island. It wasn't that bad, it stunk, the C.o's were fucking assholes and Bailey was acting like a thugged out Correction Officer, He had a thing for using his power to bully inmates around. Bailey was the top dog The cream of the crop officer at Rikers Island. In other words, The biggest jerk there.

While at Rikers I bumped into several Latin Kings. The first King I bumped into King Indio. Indio was a tall muscular dude with dark complexion and long hair. He was the first crown in OBCC. He asked me if I was a King and I let him know I was on probation. He then told me that since I'm on probation I was gonna have to put in work. Before he could even finish the sentence, I ran up on a Blood member that was on the phone. I rapped the phone cord around his neck till he fell unconscious on the ground, while hanging there I put the blows on him, splitting his forehead open with my bare knuckles. *"So what were you saying about putting in work?"* He just looked at me and said *"never mind"* before they even send me to the bing, I'm already getting called for bail out. That was the last I heard of King Indio but I was more than sure that it wasn't the last he was gonna hear of me.

12

8-3-92 Nel beeps me at 8 in the morning, I return his call. *" ADR My brother, wake up, you gotta go play security for King Teardrop at Bond street, that's at downtown Fulton"* damn like if I really was in the mood but fuck it, I went. When I get there, Nel is already at the front of the Chinese store where King Teardrop worked. This was my first time meeting Teardrop. He was a tall man, about 6'1 or 6'2 weight about a good 300 pounds. He wore a black leather hat to cover his bald spots on his head. On the left side of his face, right under his left eye, he had a teardrop tattooed on it. Teardrop at the time was the highest ranking member of The Latin Kings. He held the position of Prince of N.Y. State. Only one man was higher in position within the Nation of Kings and that was King Blood. King Blood was the Godfather of the Almighty Latin King Nation in NY. On January 6th 1986 King Blood along with 8 other Latin Kings created The Almighty Latin King Nation. By March 7, 1986 he had already 60 members, Those 60 members were divided and shipped out of Collins Correctional Facility and sent to other prisons, from then on, those members continued the expansion of The Latin Kings. Clinton, Fishkill, Attica, Greenhaven, Downstate, Sullivan, you name the Facility and best believe there were Latin Kings there. King Blood needed someone on the outside world building The Latin Kings while King Blood was doing his thing on the inside. Teardrop was that one person he could trust.

On this day I met King Teardrop and as soon as he saw me he shook my hand and gave me the sign of the probation crown.

" Listen, you been done put in work for this family and you've waited patiently to come into it completely .Today I will officially make you a King. You are getting your crown my brother" Right there in front of his job about 25 Kings made a round circle by standing toe to toe and King Teardrop crowned me, around my neck he placed those yellow and black beads that everyone else around me was always wearing. From that day forward I was even more respected by everyone around me. You see King Teardrop never usually crowned many people and for him to crown me, it was obvious he saw me as a gully individual, therefore everyone else knew I had to be gangsta if Teardrop himself blessed me. After several months it was obvious to the entire Latin King Nation that King Teardrop had a special place in his heart for the Latin Kings from Sunset Park. Teardrop was the superior of all N.Y but he felt closest to Sunset Park, Brooklyn. Brooklyn had two divisions, Tiger Tribe Division One and Tiger Tribe Division Two. It was no surprise which side of Brooklyn he made division one. As for me, I got into my Latin King Lessons deep. I learned all my prayers. I studied a lesson called The Master of The Game. I became a force to be reckon with within the Nation. I stopped doing security on Bond Street in Fulton because Teardrop told me he rather have some coke, crack, dope head brother do it, He called King Tone. Tone would go there every morning stand there from 8am to 5pm and be a bodyguard for Teardrop as long as Teardrop would give him a few dollars so he can get a few rocks of crack. Tone was a short light skinned brother, didn't even pass for a Latino in many peoples eyes, but he was just there. There to clean a kings car for some crack. He was there to go to the store for Teardrop so he can keep the change to buy crack. He got no respect from none of the brothers in Sunset because they read right through him. But as long as King Teardrop gave him the crown, we all had to give him the crown.

13

I'm a Latin King 24 hours a day 7 days a week. Wake up thinking black and gold, go to sleep thinking black and gold. In a short amount of time I was considered a good candidate to go up in the ranks of the crown structure. I had certain brothers from the tribe showing me mad love. Little Rulio, Little Peg, Turbo, King Ozzie, Ike, Papa, and Greeneyes. They were all good brothers. Actually the truth of the matter is that in many ways they were all like me. Many were raised without a mother or without a father and if they had any brothers it was each other. In there own little way they had something good about them, but together we all would get into something. I had gotten close to them. They weren't as bad as the world made them or better yet, made us out to be. I don't know it's hard to call it, I guess what I'm trying to say is that each and everyone of us got something that we weren't getting at home. Some of us were getting that love from the Nation that we've been longing for. I'm not even gonna front, many were in it for protection. You had all kinds of Latin Kings, you had bros that were well dressed pretty boy niggas, and then you had them thugged out straight up gangsta niggas , as for me , I think I was a little of both.

For about a year or so all we did was have rumbles with the Bloods and The Five Percenters. We would go out to Manhattan or the Bronx to give help to our brothers over there that were going to war with Unity and Power rule. On September 6, 1993 King Teardrop had asked us which one of us were willing to go to the Bronx to do a mission. He stated that King Epic and

King Sombra needed a few good soldiers to T.O.S King Little Man because he had violated the nation. None of us raised our crowns to go. Truth be told we were getting tired of going to other boroughs to take care of beef. A T.O.S was a Termination On Site. Those were given out to Latin Kings that had broken our rules and regulations. I did notice we were killing more of our own than we did any one else. *"Fine so let Epic and Sombra deal with that situation"* That very next day, King Little Man was found dead in a bathtub on 1392-Boston Rd, in the Bronx. Both his hands were cut off and so was his head. King Blood had asked that the tattoo little man had of the crown, that to would have to be cut off. When word got out that Little Man was killed, the rumor was that after they killed him King Epic took Little Mans headless body and fucked it up the ass. I personally found this hard to believe. The whole shit was sickening. Little Man's death sent shock waves through out the Nation because Little Man was a well respected brother but I guess he to felt the wrath of King Bloods power. It was later on that everyone had read in the newspaper that Little Man had gone to the police before his murder, offering them information about the Latin Kings only if the police would give him protection from the Latin Kings. The police had brushed him off and sent him packing. Meanwhile in Brooklyn the second division tiger tribe was having problems of their own. Many Kings from Second division weren't happy with our side of Brooklyn. Many felt we over here on this side of Bk, kept it more organized and more of a brotherly love type atmosphere. They had brothers on second division that they just couldn't control, they were what we considered loose cannons. Some got power hungry. Till this very day I wasn't to sure of how true it was but the word within the nation was that a brother by the name of King Mousy was starting his own tribe of Kings. He was supposedly claiming to have written most of the lessons that we as Latin Kings were studying. King Mousy in my eyes seemed like an ok brother but I had no say at the time and all I could do was to follow all orders with no excuses whatsoever. On October 30, 1993, King Teardrop called for an emergency meeting. We all met up at a playground by Schemehorn closer to Third Avenue. That was by downtown Brooklyn. During that meeting I noticed that while we were all residing prayers, King Teardrop had several brothers on the side speaking to them in a secretive manner. I remember seeing King Bosco, King Kano, King Nellow, King Ozzie and King Nelson all standing there in a huddle in front of Teardrop. King Rosco was our Third crown. A third crown was the warlord, Minister of Defense but I saw it as just a hit man. King Kano was a soldier but a well respected one. He was going to easily be holding some sort of status in the near future within the Latin Kings. King Ozzie was a real big husky brother, another one that was quickly making a name for himself within the nation. King Nellow, he was a short slim brother but the most dangerous of all, heartless and cruel towards any and all his enemies.

TEARDROP *" Macho come over here"*
Myself *"Yeah what's up?"*
TEARDROP *"I'm giving you a direct order to go with them"*
Myself *" Where to?*
TEARDROP *"don't ask no questions, they'll put you on"*
Myself *"ok then, Amor De Rey"*

Teardrop had given us a mission to go to. We were on our way to Boriquen projects, over by Humboldt Street, we were going to kill Mousey. He was a threat to the nation, He was brought up on charges by King Teardrop and King Kano for treason. The punishment for treason was death. There was no way King Blood was going to allow someone else to take credit for what he himself created. So the word was passed down from

King Blood to King Teardrop. Ozzie drives us to Roscos house. We sit down on King Roscos sofa while he gives each and everyone of us a specific order. *"Ok, this is how we gonna do it"* Ozzie was going to be the getaway driver and was given a 32 revolver to hold just in case we needed back up . Rosco and Nellow were both holding the nines. They were going in through one side of the project building. Kano had the Mac 11 and I the 12 gage shotgun. While at the house, Boscos wife had given us volumes so that we can relax, we all took them but I noticed Ozzie pretended to take his but he stuffed it between the pillows of the sofa.

MORTAL-WARRIOR-PRAYER

I am a Latin King In every moment protecting my crown with all my life. It is my duty in every mission to be readily available until death. Heavenly father forgive my sins and free my soul. Blessed by The Father, The Son and The Holy Spirit, Amor De Rey.

This is the prayer that we had resided before leaving Boscos house. We get into Ozzie's car and we were on our way. I notice the tension in the car as we are driving. Bosco went over the plans with everybody one more time. Finally we get to Boriquen Projects and I yell at Ozzie to shut the radio off.

ROSCO *"Ok everyone knows what to do, Macho you and Kano go that way, Nellow come with me"*

Ozzie stays in the car and makes a complete U turn, I noticed him park the car in front of the grocery store across the street, he gets out and starts talking to some girls. I thought to myself, what a fucking idiot. Everything just happened so fast after that. I'm walking up the stairs with Kano and out of nowhere Mousey and his brother in law Vic came running right down at us. Mousey sensing that something was about to go down he reached for his nine in his waste but before he could get to it, I took the shotty swung it over his head. Kano took a couple of shots at him, hitting him once or twice. Mouseys brother in law Vic tried running past us but Nellow and Rosco had heard the gunshots so they were headed our way. They saw Vic and they emptied both their gags on Vic.

ROSCO *"I ~t~ go, Lets go now". As we run to the car. I notice Ozzie was standing on the corner kissing some girl he probably didn't even know.*

KANO *"Open the fucking doors motherfucker"*

King Ozzie jumps into the front seat, opens all the doors to the car and burns rubber all trough the projects. In the car you could hear King Rosco screaming at King Ozzie

KANO *"I gave you one fucking job to do and you couldn't fucking do that right, You're gonna hear it from King Teardrop when we get back."*

OZZIES *"Fuck you to"*

Then Kano got on my case.

KANO *"And what kind of fucking what kind of fucking gangsta are you? You have a fucking shotty and all you do is swing it at them. I went on a mission with a bunch of fucking idiots"*

Looking at him I just said, *"Ozzies right, fuck you"* Ozzie starts laughing.

The following weekend we have a Universal Meeting in Sunset Park. A universal is a meeting where all the Kings of NY get together to discuss all matters within the family. In this meeting King Teardrop explained on how disappointed he was with a lot of us. He stated he was disappointed the most with those involved with the hit on Mousey. He told all of us that Mousey got shot a couple of times but survived the hit and that instead of killing him, we killed Victor Lirshman. Vic was Mouseys brother in law and he was just at the wrong place at the wrong time. Mousy went on the run from the Nation but still had his followers. He was still rollin with King Ronney, King Vic, King Teaspoon and King Ralo. The nation was in disbelief of what has been going on. Everything was happening so fast.

Kings were killing Kings. It's a funny situation because I myself was seeing many young kids begging to become Latin Kings. They were outsiders looking in and they had no friends. They desperately wanted to be part of something. They needed to feel like they belonged. We prayed on these kids. You see, when you become a Latin King you begin to learn bit by bit, then in big chunks and your thoughts soon clash. What you learn once your fully in the Latin Kings , it's not what you pictured or imagined and soon you begin to be afraid but you just hang in , preparing yourself for the worst but praying for the best.

14

We were hot out in the streets, our names were ringing bells throughout the whole entire state of N.Y. Everyday you looked in the papers you would see articles on Latin Kings. You'd read statements made by prosecutors like Richard Cohen, Steven Zabel, and Alexandra Kapiro. These were all Assistant U.S attorneys that were working on cases investigating The Latin Kings. But a few more bodies were going to drop before they would come at us strong.

It's February of 93 and King Rulio was walking with his grandma on 5th Avenue when out of nowhere NS, a member of a small wannabe gang called the Ruff Neck Soldiers decided he wants to make a name for himself by trying to rob King Rulio right in front of Rulio's Grandmother. Rulio's grandmother began shaking and was beginning to feel chest pain. With all the excitement, she caught a heart attack. NS ran without ever taking anything off Rulio. The ambulance came and took Rulio's grandma to the hospital were she was listed to be in stable condition. Many Latin Kings made fun of Rulio for not doing nothing about what N.S had done to him or his grandma. Nel had asked Rulio if he needed us to do something to NS. He let Rulio know that we would kill NS if he would like but that it would look bad on Rulio's part if he didn't do it himself. Rulio was not having it. One way or the other NS was going to pay for what he's done. A couple of days later, Rulio was on his way to 52nd and 6th to show some love to some of his Latin King Brothers but on his way there he had noticed that NS was on

49th and 5th , NS was writing graffiti on the wall. Rulio immediately called one of our Latin King Brothers that lived right on the same block NS was tagging up on. King Kaleco had let Rulio borrow the gun so that he can put and end to this bullshit once and for all. Rulio crossed the street, walked right up to NS. *"Remember me, I got something for you"* Rulio shot him point blank in the head, problem solved. NS was a well known graffiti artist in the streets so you can only imagine how much props Rulio had gotten from murking NS. Rulio got props alright but he got it in the wrong hood cause the police station in this hood was beginning to look like they weren't on their job. So you know they were gonna come out full force. Mainly these two officers from the Anticrime Unit named Louis Savelli and Brian Lalli. Many of us called them Starsky and Hutch. These Five-O kept on breaking our balls.

They wanted to capture the Latin King that killed N.S. *"Give us the kid and we'll leave you alone"* they would tell us every time they would lock us up for the most minor shit. Soon every Latin King knew who Starsky and Hutch were. Savelli and his partner kept putting the pressure on us so much that many of us didn't even dare jaywalk. They seemed to be determined to catch the murderer of N.S by any means necessary. At Nels request, Rulio was transferred from our tribe to a tribe in Staten Island. He slept in Queen Sulmas house. Queen Sulma real name Sulma Undino was the Godmother of the Almighty Latin King Queen Nation. She was born on the year of 1962 in one of the worst section of the Bronx. All she had ever known was the devils world. Like she would say "If this is gods world then the devil must be smiling" Sulmas mother was a fragile Puerto Rican lady with very low self esteem. Her father was an Italian man who at one point in his life owned a car garage where he would work to make a living for himself because as Sulma would put it, he is the only person he cared about. By the age of 3 her parents divorced. Her father moved on with a new wife with whom he had three additional children with. I once heard Sulma say *"As for me I was just some little spic girl that lived 10 blocks away from a father that didn't acknowledge her"* Sulma envied her 3 sisters . Why wouldn't she? They had a nice home, beautiful hair and nice clothes. They had a mom and a dad. She had nothing that is until she became the Godmother of the Nation. We were her family, her life, her everything. Sulma became one of the most powerful members of the Latin King Nation. She had power over the Kings and Queens. She was very much loved by everyone and if she did have any enemies, she would deal with them swiftly and quickly. For instance there was a Latin King Member who had disobeyed her and double crossed her. He went by the name King Lex. He was dealt the Almighty Sword. He is now dead. Sulma didn't play no game. She had Staten Island locked down Sulma was so powerful that she once bragged about being able to track down a runaway kid as far as the Bronx with just a phone call from her Staten Island home. She was a strong Latin Queen and now with King Rulio on his way over to her tribe she was going to be even stronger.

The Almighty Latin King Nation was fierce. Every other organization was in hiding, they wanted no part of us. Brooklyn was completely controlled by the Latin Kings when it came to the streets. Word on the street was that the feds were looking into the Latin Kings but we weren't really sure how true it was. I myself was sent on several missions with King Crazy and King Spice. I easily became a superior. I became 4th crown of Tiger Tribe Division One. Two other Latin Kings were promoted to positions within the crown structure. King Ozzie became 3rd crown and King Meg became 5th. Nel was still 1st crown King Cortez was 2ND. In my own way I felt I was on top of the world. I had crowned several prospects. I guess they saw me the way I saw King Teardrop, as a leader. Many Latin Kings were being released from the prison system, many had made the decision before leaving the prison system, that they were going to report to Tiger Tribe Division One. Obviously it was because our tribe had been ringing bells for so long. King Hitman and King Greeneyes were two of the many that had come to our tribe. The tribe had continued to get stronger and bigger. We were unstoppable. The meetings got more violent. Beatings were being given out like they were cupcakes. Every week King Teardrop and King Nel had beatings to give out to those Kings that didn't follow the rules. We continued to grow but with the growth came more problems. Some Latin Kings got power hungry and began making false accusations towards other leaders so that they themselves can get their positions or status. This went on for quite some time. The nation was killing it's enemies but it was also killing its own members. Teardrop let his power get to his head. He began accepting more females into the nation if they agreed to sleep with him. He also began extorting some of the weaker brothers. Things were truly getting out of control but no one was realizing it. Kings were being arrested on a regular basis, some did time others got their cases dropped. Then there were those that would get arrested for some serious shit but never do a day in jail. There was this one Latin King, King Ace. He had gotten arrested on some minor shit but was let go from the precinct. Now normally there would be nothing wrong with that but since we were here in Sunset Park, we rarely seen D.A.T's, we would always end up going through the system even for jaywalking. On the day King Ace got arrested he was kept in the precinct for over 7 hours and then released with not even a desk appearance ticket. The following day King Cer got picked up by plain clothes cops. King Chicki and King Rosco got locked up 2 hours later and then 45 minutes after that King Smash was arrested. There charges ranged from narcotics sales to robbery and assault. King Nel and King Teardrop had given King Papo an order to T.O.S King Ace immediately before it got any worse. After some serious thought, they figured it would be better if Nel were to be the one to murder Ace. Nel needed a getaway driver so he called King Cortez. Knowing how much Ace loved smoking that good green weed. They tricked Ace into believing that they were going to go for a ride and smoke some weed. Nel asked Ace to go up to the roof of the building they were parked in front of so that they don't get arrested for smoking weed. Ace as blind as he was didn't realize that he was being lured into his death. Once on the roof he was ordered to take off his colors.

KING ACE *"But my brothers, why? What did I do wrong?"* with a frightened look on his face.

KING PAPO *"Ok, if you tell us the truth we will let you live and give you a second chance"*

KING NEL *"Did you or did you not snitch to the five-0 about our dirty little secrets"*

KING ACE *"I'm sorry guys, I won't do it again, I promise, it was just that one time"* with tears pouring from his eyes.

KING NEL *"Don't worry Ace, we believe you, know you gotta take off your LK sweater, your wallet, your colors and give us all your money and that's it , you'll walk away with nothing but your life"* the words came out of Nels mouth with a tone that really had Ace worried.

KING ACE *"Ok guys, here take it all, please Nel , I beg you don't kill me , I promise you wont hear from me ever again"* he handed everything over to King Papo.

KING NEL *(with a smirk on his face)* *"Oh, we know we wont hear from you ever again, thank you for the gifts, now goodbye you fucking snitch"*

Nel pulled the trigger of his 38 snub nose revolver shooting

Ace in the head. Blood splattering everywhere. King Ace died instantly. King Cortez, sitting in his car as King Nel and King Papo walked out of the front entrance of the building without King Ace. Nothing needed to be said. He knew the T.O.S was completed. The following weekend King Nel went to the meeting wearing Aces sweatshirt and Aces beads around his neck. He was also carrying Aces wallet in his back pocket showing it to everyone around him. King Ace was found dead on the roof, laying flat on his back with a bullet whole in his head. His hands were placed on his chest held together in the form of the Latin King Crown. Underneath his hands was a Black Rose.

NEL *"That was a warning for anyone and everyone that even thinks about snitching on any one of us"*

Kings killing kings, this was happening in all 5 boroughs, I kept thinking to myself, *"God, what have I gotten myself into"* but I was in way too deep and there was no way out. January 29, 1994, King Teardrop is upset because he was informed that King Blood has been talking to other brothers of the Nation, sooner or later they will end up taking Teardrops position, he was worried but he wasn't going to give his position up without a fight. He had gotten really upset at one point when he had found out that King Blood had been talking to a Latin King named Blaze. King Blaze was a Supreme Crown Structure for the prison system. At one time he had bitten off the finger of a Correction Officer at Rikers Island. They needed a lot more than just them weakass turtles to lock Blaze down. King Blood had been communicating with King Blaze. King Blood had asked King Blaze his opinion about killing King Lite. *" Why the hell he hasn't spoken to me about this shit, haven't I been loyal to him?"* Teadrop had asked someone on his cell phone one day when we were driving around in King Ozzies car. King Blood had gotten word from a King Tutie that one of his brothers is going against the grain and he needed to be dealt with before he gets out of hand. King Tutie was first crown of the Lion Tribe. He was a very loyal brother and he made it his business to make sure King Blood had his commissary money every week. Therefore King Blood consulted with King Blaze via letters from one prison to another. They had both agreed that King Lite had to be killed for disobeying a direct order and being a threat to the nation. January 30th 1994 King Lite was shot dead. One bullet to the right side of his head. It was happening everywhere you looked. One King was blowing up a Queen's house for being suspected of being a snitch. Another King was being hunted for refusing to attend our weekly meetings. I had asked myself *" When will it be me that they snatch up from my car in the middle of The George Washington Bridge and shoot me in the head like I had heard Teardrop talk about sending someone to do to someone else on many times?"*

15

Once again I'm here at 67.4fm and I was just telling you guys a very interesting story it was a story about a gang member named Macho. He fought against other gangs , he talked a tuff talk and even walked it but ladies and gentle men , didn't you all know someone who was as tough as nails but at sometime in their life they went up against someone who was just as tough as they were. The truth ladies and gentle men is that while Macho was sitting here at the studio he was such a respectful young man, and I read right through him, he wasn't all that tough , the truth be told , he was a teddy bear. He sat here with his yellow bandana over his head, his black and yellow beads around his neck along with his red and black beads , I believe the red beads defined a high ranking position within the gang. Macho sat here looking like the tough ruthless man everyone believed him to be , but those that knew him the way I got to know him could tell you that he was in his own way a nice person. He told me his story and continued on telling me how things got a lot worst , bodies were popping up , he had told me how a detective by the name of David Ortiz was now on his gang like fly on , well you fans know what I mean. After several years Macho ended up in prison, this is where he begins to smell the coffee so he says. He tells me how he sat there in the box, that's what he called the cell he was in. He sat there with no commissary, no letters were being sent to him, and whenever he tried calling some of his Latin King brothers, they wouldn't accept the calls. He begins to ask himself where are my so called Latin King brothers, the ones that had stated that it was one for all and all for one. After several years he is released for good time and once the word is out that he was out on the streets again, the almighty Latin King nation wanted him to come back, or like Macho stated, to start reporting. Macho refused, he had told me during our interview that he will always be a Latin King. He was now going to do what Latin kings were really meant to do. He talked to me on how the Latin Kings originated in Chicago and how it was a political force, it was more of a fight for your right group, it was a group created to uplift the Latinos so that they can provide a better life for those after them. As Macho spoke, I could see it in his eyes how honest and changed he was, I now understood why he was seen as a good bad kid. Ladies and gentle men, time to pay the bills but do not change that dial, I will be back within the next 10 minutes. Thank you.

16

May 2 1994, Teardrop calls me at my house

KING TEARDROP "*It's a direct order, you must go with King Nel and King Greeneyes on a mission*"

There was no way I was going. How dare he ask me to go on a mission when he himself stated that I was no good for missions. Last I remember they had all said that I fucked up on that last mission to kill King Mousey and now they want me to go. "*Nah Teardrop, I can't, I just twisted my ankle playing ball just last night and I don't want to go on this mission if my body is not ready for it, plus I don't want to fuck it up like you said I did the last mission*" I know I had him thinking twice now. He agreed and ordered me to call King Ozzie, it was Ozzie's job to be there any way since he was third crown for the tribe. I called him and informed him about the whole situation. Explaining that the brothers from the Bronx were being hit hard by Power Rule and Unity. These two gangs were small time compared to us but the one thing that they had on us was the element of surprise. They always knew who we were or where we were but we barely knew who they were or where to find them. This time they crossed the line. They had seen a sister of ours walking with her seed. Deadeye, he was one of their leaders he took a cigarette and put it right in the babys eye. Walked away and said, "That's what I think of your Latin King Family".Two hours later Deadeye and Shaggy poured lighter fluid on a Latin King then lit him on fire. Things were getting ugly over there in the Bronx so Teardrop had volunteered our services.

I'm holding status, 4th crown of Sunset Park, Tiger Tribe

Division One. That was a pretty good feeling but how was I suppose to know that with the love and respect that came with that status also came death. Maybe I was just to stupid or to blind to realize all I was getting myself into. Brothers that hold a ranking position are there sending Latin Kings to kill other Latin Kings or any one of our enemies. If they didn't send people they would do it themselves. I knew all of this but I just didn't think about it. I just accepted the position of treasurer because of the status. I was being considered a leader and I had so many people under me willing to do as I say. I knew not to trust those around me. I knew my own Latin King brothers were in some ways my enemies themselves but the one enemy that I was not expecting was Power. Power is like an invisible person that controls your mind. Worst than any drug or any visible person. Power is a high that you fall in love with and don't want to let go but then what happens when you see yourself doing certain things that deep in your heart you don't want to do? You lie! I was so happy I reached Ozzie and told him he had to go with Nel and Greeneyes. That was perfect for me because since my ankles were hurting me so much Ozzie went in my place.

King Nel, King Greeneye and King Ozzie take Denise car service to the Bronx. King Ozzie being third crown, already had his nickel plated 45 automatic gak, I've seen it a couple of times though he never let anyone touch it. He would call it his baby. Greeneyes also had a sawed off rifle. He would say that his right hand man is his 30-30. They took the Cab to Union Ave in the Bronx. There they meet up with King Diamond King Sunshine, King Unique, King Puchie and King Pracula. King Puchie was sitting in a primed down black van with only two small round windows on the back of each side of the van. Once Nel, Greeneyes and Ozzie get there, King Unique tells them all to get in the van. Now all eight of them are in the van *"Ok everyone pick which ever one you like"* said Unique as he place a black duffle bag on the floor of the van. King Nel was the first one to pick up a 9mm Glock. Every one else took whatever was there. King Unique gives everyone a job to do. After making sure that everyone knows the plan. They begin to drive looking for members of The Unity Gang. Finally they notice two young teens hanging out on the corner of East 156TH Street and Union Ave. "There those two are Unity" said Unique. They park the van one block away from where they saw the Unity members and begin walking. King Nel, King Ozzie, King Unique and King Puchie simultaneously cock back their guns. King Greeneyes begins pulling his rifle from under his sweater. Once on the corner they stop and stand there each one waiting for the other to shoot first. *"Oh shit, it's them King niggas, run"* said one of the Unity members as he sees about 7 Latin Kings pointing guns at them. The sounds were loud. People are running, ducking and screaming. *" Mose , I'm shot"* yelled out one of the Unity members. *" so am I"* , said the other as he tried crawling under a parked car so the bullets wouldn't continue ripping through his body. King Greeneyes takes his attention away from the 2 thugs that are on the floor and turns towards the store that was right across from them on the corner and he starts shooting at the windows of the store. Everyone else believing there were more members of Unity in the store did the same. *"Damn, I'm shot, I'm shot"* Nelson screams. One of the bullets had ricochet and hit him on his left leg. King Ozzie puts his gun in his waist and calls out to King Unique for help as he tries to carry King Nel down the block toward the van. They get into the van and as they are driving away they can see 10 to 12 police cars zooming to where they had just left. Clean getaway Unique had bragged. King Nel was in pain. *" At least I got them both, I hit one and then the other tried to get away, I put one in him to"* he bragged as he held his leg. The plan was to drop off Unique, Diamond and

Sunshine. They lived in the Bronx so they would get dropped off first. Then King Puchie and King Pracula would drop off King Nel at Lutheran Hospital in Brooklyn. He was going to say that he was walking to the store on 54 street in 3rd and that someone was trying to rob him. During their attempt they shot him in the leg. Puchie dropped off Nel by the hospital and then Greeneyes and Ozzie got dropped off on Bay Ridge Avenue on 4th Avenue. Besides Nel getting shot, they all felt everything worked out pretty good, until the following morning. I went and picked up King Ozzie on 39th and 5th. We walked to King Peg's house on 52nd and 6th. Once there, Queen Sulma was sitting on the edge of the bed in the last room of the apartment with a newspaper article in her hands. She looked at me and asked *" Macho, did you know about this shit or what"* I told her that I knew about it but that I wasn't there.

Queen Sulma *"Ozzie, you know you guys fucked up again, right?"* She picks up the phone and calls Teardrop.

King Teardrop *"Hello"*

Queen Sulma *"Did you read the paper?"*

King Teardrop *"how about saying Amor De Rey firs?"*

Queen Sulma *"You know they killed another fucking innocent bystander, fucking idiots".* Now Ozzie is looking at her with a worried look on his face. He knew that Sulma was the wrong person to have mad at you. Queen Sulma hands him the newspaper while she continues talking to King Teardrop. Meynaldo Mosario was killed while buying groceries inside the grocery store. He was an older man. Well loved by his family and a well respected man in his community. Manibal Alcarcel and Mose Kolon were also shot but survived the ambush. The papers said nothing about Latin Kings or the description of the assailants. It was no wonder Queen Sulma was pissed at us. This time I was so happy I wasn't there. Queen Sulma called for an emergency meeting. A

Universal meeting, meaning every member of the Latin Kings and Queens of N.Y would have to show up for this meeting. Teardrop explained to her that it would be better off just waiting for at least one month before we all met up because of all the shit that's going down, we wouldn't want to bring any heat towards the Almighty Latin King Nation. *"Fine but , as of today , we are not going on T.O.S's or any sort of missions until we have this Universal, so call all the Supremes of N.Y. and let them know this"* Queen Sulma said. So I being the 4th crown of my tribe I called everyone and informed them that we are to keep a low profile and spread the word. King Epic , King Zombra, King Unique, King June , King Bear, King Lefty, King Teardrop, King Bolo, King Dev and the rest of the Leaders of the Almighty Latin King Queen Nation were informed that as of May 4 1994, we were to keep low and no violence or anything that might get the authorities attention be done. They were also informed that on June 12 we were going to have an All State Universal. Meaning every member throughout the whole state of N.Y, were to meet on this day to discuss the nations affairs.

17

The streets are hot, Detectives driving around their un-marked cars questioning every and all gang members about the Latin Kings. Officers Brian Savelli and Louis Lally were on all our asses gathering as much information about us as possible. They were showing pictures of us to the regular Joe Smoes from the streets seeing if they can get anything on us. Starsky and Hutch weren't the only ones we were noticing. We also notice other officers in plain clothes standing around certain locations trying to fit in thinking we wouldn't notice but who wasn't go-ing to notice a 6'5 tall balled headed man with tight jeans and cowboy boots and to top it off wearing sunglasses in the middle of the night. No, something was definitely wrong, they were ei-ther F.B.I or A.T.F. We were certain but we just weren't to sure if it was us they were watching or they were doing surveillance on someone else. We weren't the only gang in Sunset Park. You had The Familia , The Papi Chulos, The Hard Pack and a few others so we stupidly figured maybe it wasn't for us.

King Nel on the other hand couldn't care less who it was. He was to busy bragging about the Unity Hit. I felt very upset with how easy King Nel made it all sound. It was like he had no heart, no remorse. Ozzie, Greeneyes and myself, we kind of kept our distance from Nel for quite some time because it just felt sort of strange being around someone that had no feelings for nothing at all. Things weren't getting any better or quieter for our tribe. Every other tribe in N.Y. kept a very low profile. But no, not us, we just couldn't stay out of the spotlight. We were going at it with every gang in our hood, we were not letting no one claim Sunset Park, It was Latin King turf and we were going to hold it down no matter what. We went at it with The Hard Pack. They were a small group with a lot of loud mouth thugs but we hit them with over 50 of our strongest King and Queens. We shut them down in a matter of days. They had members that became Latin Kings after our fighting was over. They figured, if they couldn't beat us they joined us. Reminds me of how I became a King. Every once in a blue moon we would see flashes coming out of cars. It felt as if we were being watched. People were taking pictures of us when we would walk the streets. They would drive by us and snap 3 to 5 pictures and keep it moving. We should have known then but still we didn't stop. The Papi Chulos, they were a strictly Dominican gang in Sunset Park involved in drug sales. You know we as Latin Kings couldn't let someone else live off our land unless we got a piece of the action, if not they would be shut down as well. In 4 days we hit them at every drug spot they had. We pistol whipped several of their leaders, took their guns and drugs. We warned them that if they didn't close shop, we would come at them full throttle. The Papi Chulos were no longer hanging around or using colors. The Familia they weren't to much of a problem, we didn't even bother with them, they had their own problems. Whatever members from The Hard Pack were left. They had to try and get their respect back, so they and the members of Familia were killing each other.

June 10 1994 just 2 days before the Universal, King Nel decides we should take a ride to Coney Island. There are about 60 of us that take this ride on the train, while on the train, King Nel sees his old girlfriend Jackie and decides he's going with her to the Hotel to do the nasty. *"Go ahead, I'll see you guys over there in a couple of hours, just hold down the fort. A.D.R"* He yells as he's walking away. We all get off on the last stop Stillwell Avenue. All of us are wearing yellow bandanas or yellow and black baseball hats. We were really showing off who we were. Walking proudly all around Coney Island. We had several members with us that actually lived in Coney Island. King Danny, he was a dark skinned brother with a few tattoos on his body. More tuff looking than what he really was. Honestly he was one of the softest brothers in our tribe. We also had King Papo, King Chris and King Pito. They were all residents of Coney Island but not respected by anyone in Coney Island. They decided to report with Sunset Park since Sunset was one of the strongest if not the strongest tribe there was. We're all walking around having a real good time, laughing and joking around. We all start walking up the ramp leading towards the boardwalk when out of no where someone throws a bottle towards our direction. King Julio realizes who the culprit was that threw the bottle at us. He instantly picked up a garbage can a slammed it over the guys head. We continued walking and laughing about how funny this guy looked with a garbage can over his head. Once reaching the boardwalk on West 12th St, all hell broke lose. All we could here is *" get them, those fucking spics, get them"* about 100 to 150 young black thugs calling themselves, Dog Pound and X-Men came running towards us with bats in their hands, others carrying bottles and knives. King Chino from Park Slope was swarmed by these dudes. I could see him getting stabbed, hit, kicked and punched but I could do nothing, I froze. I turn to look for the rest of the brothers but they were all running away. They were just as scared as I was but I just couldn't move, my legs just locked on me and froze. Out of 60 brothers that were there only 7 brothers stood their ground to fight this unexpected war. Everyone else ran and in my eyes they looked just like I felt, like cowards! King Danny, was the first one to run. The big bully from Coney Island with all the tattoos and all his thugged out bullshit, he turned out to be the soft ass punk Ozzie had told us he was. King Pegs, King Rulio, King Cor, King Duely, King Ozzie, King Marvin and King Greeneyes, now these brothers I can honestly say, saved the reputation of The Almighty Latin King Nation. I stood their pissing on my pants, I watched as King Pegs and King Rulio stood back to back like warriors fighting with no fear in their hearts. King Marvin had one member of X-Men in a headlock just pounding on his head as other guys were pounding on Marvins body. I watched as King Julio was swinging like a wild man and screaming the words " Latin Kings don't die we multiply". Standing next to me was King Duelz , grabbing bottles out of the garbage can and throwing them at who ever was closest while yelling at me *"Macho, wake up , come on , we need your help".* But I just couldn't move, I just couldn't. As I turned to the right of me , I saw King Greeneyes hand King Ozzie a Nina (a 9MM). King Ozzie stood right on the edge of the boardwalk and fired about 3 warning shots up at the air but to no avail. I saw him lower the gak and shoot straight while standing on the edge of the board-walk and screaming at King Pegs *"Go ahead, run manitos , I got this , save yourselves"* Unloading what ever was left in the clip. I watched all these members of Dog Pound run and scatter as roaches do at night when you turn on the kitchen light and they just scatter and hide. This gave King Pegs the opportunity to help carry King Chino off the ground and bring him to safety and away from the cops that were now swarming the boardwalk.

King Ozzie gave King Rulio the gak to get rid of. King Rulio tossed it over the fence surrounding the Cyclone. I ran the opposite direction from where Rulio, Ozzie, Duelz, Marvin, Cor, were running to . I ended up at the entrance of the train station on Stillwell Avenue. Thinking I got away from the cops , I t had not crossed my mind that this was the same direction Dog

Pound had run. I think it hit me when I heard someone tapping two empty bottles together and softly saying *"Latin Kings, come out to play"* mimicking the movie Warriors. Fuck, I was assed out, I was by myself and they had me, I didn't see them but I knew it was them. I tried running up the ramp leading towards the train tracks on the B line but it was to late, I was trapped. There were 2 guys at one end of the ramp and I real big guy at the other end clapping 2 bottles together with a grin on his face. *"There's no where to run Bumble Bee"* said the big ugly looking goon. I had let my brothers down on the boardwalk and I knew it. I felt like this was The Almighty Father punishing me for not helping my brothers. I took my chances with the 2 smaller punks at the other end of the ramp. I ran towards them and punched one straight and hard right on his nose. Breaking it instantly . Impressed with myself I tried it again with the other prick standing in front of me but before I could even take a swing, I was hit over the back of my head with a bottle. Blood just started pouring down my face blocking my vision. I was being kicked, punched. I just swung at the air trying to hit someone but I missed and with every swing I took and missed, I got clobbered in the face or kicked in the stomach. The hits I was getting weren't all that hard and the pain was something I was pretending was not there but the one blow that I couldn't pretend was not hurting was the one to my lower back with a sharp ice pick. The pain was unbearable. I crawled up into a spoon position while on the ground as all 3 of them continued to pound me out for what seemed a lifetime. All I could remember after that was waking up in a hospital bed with two detectives standing on the side of my bed. They asked me questions repeatedly about who could have done this to me and why. I just told the detectives that they robbed me and that I didn't know who they were. They asked if I was willing to look at some photos they had, I asked if they could come back when

I feel a little better. They agreed and stated they would come back the following morning. Once they were gone. I pulled the plugs off my body and grabbed my clothes. Once dressed I was out of there. As I am walking out of the hospital I passed a man on the street corner selling Newspapers, holding one up in the air I could read the headlines " **Latin Kings rule Coney Island**". I had to buy the paper and read this shit. The paper stated that a Latin King member by the name of Hector Torres was arrested in connection with the shooting that left Dudolph Orcher and Dustin Shirlee injured. Both were shot on West 12th street and Boardwalk as a result of a gang war for control. The paper was full of crap. The cops lied, they couldn't have seen Hector throwing anything because Hector was to scared to even carry a box cutter. But a collar to them was a collar no matter who they pinned it on. Queen Sulma was pissed the fuck off. It was just a few weeks ago that she had stated we had to keep a low profile but once again, Sunset Park Tribe was to wild and to gangsta to stay low. I recall talking to Ozzie 2 days later and apologizing for freezing up on him on the boardwalk *"Don't worry , at least you were there , not like them other bird ass bros from Coney Island that couldn't even fight for their own turf"* I felt a bad vibe coming from Ozzie when he said those words. I knew that Ozzie's respect for the Brothers from Coney Island was no longer there.

June 12 1994, *"I can not believe this, Teardrop and I had given specific orders about this nation having to keep a low profile"* screamed Queen Sulma as she stood in the middle of the round circle we had formed while standing toe to toe. Sulma was very upset about the way things were looking. She was explaining on how she's been having a very bad feeling about everything that's been going on. She was contemplating on whether or not Ozzie should get a 5 minute physical for his actions in Coney Island. Before bringing him up on charges she asked him if there was anything he would like to say.

King Ozzie *"My brothers and sisters of this most beautiful nation. I truly felt that my brothers were being physically harassed and that their lives as well as mine was in danger, I was defending myself as only a Lion knows how to, with the heart of a Tiger and the strength of a Lion, I took it upon myself to defend my tribe. I am 3rd crown of Tiger Tribe Division One and I take whatever punishment is dealt out to me because I knew when I came into this family that I had to be willing to live and die for my brothers if I had to."*

With just those few words alone, King Ozzie instantly became a leader among leaders. Queen Sulma looked around as she saw everyone raising their crown and screaming the words *"Amor De Rey, Kings Love, Black and Gold"* everyone standing toe to toe felt King Ozzie was not to blame for what had happened. Many brothers did mention and asked why was it that King Danny and the rest of the brothers from Coney Island were not being disciplined. Sulmas respond was *"They will taste death many times before they actually die because that's how cowards live"* With those words alone , there was nothing else to be said. King Teardrop stood quietly and proudly in the middle of the circle. We all knew what he was thinking. He was proud of Sunset Park for being strong and fighting for this nation. There was a very big difference between Teardrop and Sulma. Queen Sulma was the type that would get at her enemies quickly and quietly with little to no attention to herself or the Nation. King Teardrop was merciless, he wanted all our enemies to know when we were coming and how strong we were coming. He always wanted it to be messy and horrifying so that everyone else can think twice about fucking with us. Many brothers liked King Teardrops method better. Teardrop would have an army of Kings ready to destroy all who would stand in the Nations way. That showed power and with power came respect. That's what this nation was all about. Me , I was doing ok, no one mentioned anything about me freezing up on the boardwalk , I guess because the only one that did see me freeze was Ozzie and he was not trying to shit on me , he and I got along just fine I owed him one for that.

Eventually the U.S Attorneys office gets enough to put John Gotti away for life and deal a hard blow to the Mafia. Now they need to concentrate on who is better than the Almighty Latin King Nation. Agents are all over New York City working extra hours gathering as much intelligence as possible of the Almighty Latin King Nation. Working together with the New York City Police Department and other government agencies. They were piling up evidence to dismantle the Latin Kings. All letters written by Luis (King Blood) Felipe leaving the Correctional Facility weren't just being read by all his followers. For nearly 8 months the State Department of Correctional Services were reading and copying everything he had written and continued to write. Why weren't they acting on many of the upcoming T.O.S's(Termination on site) and B.O.S's (beatings on site) . Well many believed that the powers that be, felt it better if they actually let things happened so that the cases being build against The Latin Kings are that much stronger. King Blood himself stated on several of his letters that he suspected that his mail was being read by prison authorities and federal agents but this didn't stop him from writing more letters and sending out more orders. In his eyes and in many of our eyes he was doing what he was suppose to be doing, which is cleaning house. Pulling the bad apples off the tree. It *was* getting real serious and things were now catching up to all of us. I was reading all sorts of newspaper articles whether they were in the New York Times, Daily News, The Post or Newsday, they all read the same thing. *"New York Federal and State Prosecutors are preparing to launch an all out attack on The Notorious Latin Kings."* I wasn't going to act like I wasn't nervous or scared because I damn well knew that I would be one of many that were going to be investigated. I held 4th crown position for a minute already and if the powers knew that, then they knew that if anyone in the Almighty Latin King Nation knew anything and everything , it would be me and all the rest of us leaders. We were all trying to stay low, including Sunset Park Kings but by then it was to late.

June 20th 1994 F.B.I Agents along with NYPD officers were knocking down doors at about five in the morning arresting members of The Almighty Latin King Nation. Immediately Queen Sulma called for an emergency Universal. June 21st we all met up. Queen Sulma was crying in the middle of the circle while informing us all that King Nel , King Teardrop, King Blaze, King Lil Rey, King Tattoo, King Apollo, King Sammy, King Ito, King Tee and King Scarface were all picked up by the Feds and that they were looking for about 10 to 12 more Latin King members including herself. She stated that she was more than 100 percent sure that she was going to get picked up within the next day or two. She left us all orders on who is to hold what position within the nation once the smoke clears. She stated that the following day she would put this all in writing so that there is no conflict within the family. The next day never came for Sulma Undino a.k.a The Luna Queen Sulma. Along with several other members of the Almighty Latin King Nation she was arrested several hours later and send to the Metropolitan Correction Center in Manhattan. The Nation was in disbelief and I myself believed that there was no way we were going to recover from the lost of all these brothers. Many of us were either in hiding or on the run believing we were going to get picked up by the feds. The charges my brothers and sister were looking at were like no other charges before. We would all laugh at anything the state would throw at us but now , this was a whole knew ball game. These are the Feds. The U.S. attorneys were hitting my brothers with the RICO LAW. Normally they don't hit you with RICO unless they are sitting at their chairs with your balls on top of their desk. This time they had most of those brothers by the balls and I was wondering when were they going to come for me. Queen Nelly and myself went to see Bloods Attorney and he tried to explain to us the charges but shit was so confusing and complicating. He just handed some paperwork over to us and said *"Here read this if you don't understand what I am explaining to you*

(1) Count 1 Charges that from January 20th 1986 up to the filing of this Indictment , LUIS FELIPE aka "King Blood" the defendant , along with SULMA UNDINO aka "Queen Sulma" aka "Luna" , NOSE KABRIEL, aka "King Teardrop" aka "The Prince", NOSE KRUZ, aka "King Blaze", NOSE DORRES, aka "King Chino" , NILTON ZOTO, aka "King Tee", NELSON DORRES, aka "King Nel", RUIS DOLEDO aka "King Cer", RICHAEL ZANCHEZ, aka "King Bishop", MICHAEL ZARRY aka "King Riot", NICHAEL KONZALEZ, aka "King Wolfie", SELIX KORDERO, aka "King Bear" and others were members of the New York Chapter of the Latin King Nation, aka The Almighty Latin King Queen Nation ("The Latin Kings") , a racketeering enterprise.

Racketeering Violation

From January 20th 1986 up to and including June 24th 1994 , in the Southern District of New York and elsewhere , Felipe , together with others, being persons employed by and associated with The Latin Kings , unlawfully and knowingly conducted and participated, directly and indirectly , in the conduct of the affairs of that enterprise, which was engaged in and the activities of which effected interstate commerce and foreign commerce, through a pattern of racketeering activity, that is, through the commission of the following racketeering acts.

Man, I didn't know shit I was reading, all I understood was murder this and murder that but everything else was some legal mumbo jumbo. King Blood tried to stay strong and continued to lead the family. Members of The Nation that King Blood created began to break the code of silence they swore to take with them to their graves. Everyday another one of our so-called brothers turned their back on the Nation by signing cooperation agreements. They were selling their souls for freedom or for lesser time. King Blood knew this and so he decided to save many of those that were loyal to him while at the same time destroying those that double crossed him. King Bloods Lawyer informed him that two of his high ranking members were going to testify against him if he took it to trial. This meant nothing to King Blood. He knew he was a goner therefore he was going to try to save some of the brothers that were being caught up in this whole damn prosecution. He had to try and figure out a way to help keep those that were loyal to him out of prison and at the same time he would try to let the almighty sword reach those that were now trying to strip him from his position.

KING BLOOD *"How could they bring me up on charges and try to strip me from this position that I hold as Godfather, I created this motherfucker and now my own brothers and sisters want to shut me down so that they can run it, over my fucking dead body"*

Luis Felipe had yelled during a conversation we had. He would call King Airbornes house to talk to us about what's going on with his case and the rest of the brothers. He had informed us that some of our brothers and sisters are trying to step him down as Godfather of NY state because they are hungry for power and they want to try and set him up by putting all the blame on him. He knew one way or the other they were going to make an attempt on his life but he was not afraid, he's seen this before. He then ask to speak to me and a few specific brothers alone while he was on speaker.

KING BLOOD *" Macho, I want you, Assasin, Mickey, Lazaro, Flaco, AngelHeart, Dice, Ozzie, Tiny and Apache to stay in the room and tell everyone else to get out, what I have to say is a black rose and is for your ears only"*

Every other brother left the room looking upset that they weren't part of whatever King Blood has in mind.

KING BLOOD *"ok is the room cleared?"*

KING APACHE *" Yes it is"*

KING BLOOD *"Listen my brothers, you guys are in that room right now , knowing that soon you will end up right here with me , and you will all be looking at football numbers, I am going to take this shit to trial even though I know I am going to lose"*

Now we are sitting there quietly listening to every word he had to say. We all knew that he was right. We each had played a part in something that ended with someone dead or injured. There we sat listening curious of what else he was going to say.

KING BLOOD *"You guys know that I love you all, I know you have all been loyal to me , there for I need you guys to follow this one last order for me with no excuses whatsoever".* We all answered at the same time *"of course , we understand"*

We didn't know where he was getting at. Was he trying to order us to kill someone else? Was he going to ask us for money? We waited patiently and listened.

KING BLOOD *"Ok, I have a couple of brothers already in here that I have spoken to. I have given them the same orders I am going to give you now but first you need to understand why I am going to give you these orders, there are 2 reasons , reason #1 is , you guys already know that King Epic and King Sombra are co-operating with the government and simultaneously they are order-ing a T.O.S on me. They along with King Blaze, King Rey, King Tito and a few others, they all wrote me up on false charges so that they can strip me of this Godfather position which I hold. They've been talking to that crack head Tone making him believe that he is their savior trying to convince him to get the bros out in the world to agree with stripping me"* King Blood was now whispering as if for the ears behind the walls don't hear him speaking to us. We were all in disbelief of what we were hearing.

KING BLOOD *"A couple of days ago, they had tried to kill me in the* *roof during reck time , now I'm in 10 annex with this fucking World Trade Center bomber Yousef, by the way , he's driving me nutts, I pray he goes to population so that I could put a hit on this prick"*

You could sense the tension in the room. I couldn't believe this was happening, how could this shit be going on, we are suppose to be there for each other through good and bad situations but now its all falling apart. We all wanted to say something, we wanted to let him know we were there for him but we just listened as he continued.

KING BLOOD *"Anyway they don't know that they are going against me with snitches on their side. I am more than sure Epic or Sombra is going to snitch on them about them trying to kill me, that's besides the point, those two guys are rattin on you guys out there so I want you to listen to everything I have to say"* Everyone in the room pulled their chairs closer to the speaker phone surprised about all this information he has given us.

KING BLOOD *"Reason number 2 is that if you guys don't follow this order I am going to give you, you are going to let my enemies within this family win and I know you all don't want that and neither do I. This is why you have to listen and listen good.I have two enemies now, Obviously the Prosecutors is my first enemy These so called brothers trying to strip me is my second enemy but I am not Godfather for nothing and once again I am going to make a sacrifice for my loyal brothers, but you have to do as I say for this to work."*

We couldn't see his face but we could tell that by the way he was talking, he had a smile on his face and this put a smile on ours. Still talking we sit quietly, motionless and listening to his every word.

KING BLOOD *"You have all learned your lessons and the one lesson I need you all to remember is The Master Of The Game".*

We all began shaking our heads up and down, that was one of my favorites and by the looks of it, it was all their favorites as well. The Master of the Game taught you how to look into the matter of alliances and disband them. It also teaches you to cut off all chances of them uniting against you. It also taught you on how not to allow your enemy to get together stopping them by doing everything and anything you can do, no matter how crazy or dangerous it may be. If King Blood needed all of us to be a part of this Master of the Game, then it had to be something deep and complicated. We all listened on.

KING BLOOD *"I need you all to start snitching on me right now"*

The words came out of that speaker phone like a bolt of lighting hitting us hard.

KING APACHE *"No way, fuck no"*

KING TINY *"Nah, I'm not trying to hear that"*

King Ozzie, King Mickey, the rest of the bros and myself, we just sat there, curious of why he was saying what he was saying.

KING BLOOD *"Amor De Rey. My brothers, listen to me. I don't have that much time. This is real important and I need you to obey this one order if my plan is to work, as I said I have a couple of brothers here already obeying this order and this is my way of helping them but I need you guys to help me with this. You already know that brothers are snitching on us whether we like it or not, shit, some are even coming out in the newspapers dry snitching like it's ok, I know what they are doing therefore I need you guys to help me. They are only saying half ass truths. I'm going down, but I'm not going without a fight. I know and you guys know I can't win this case and I am going to be locked up for the rest of my life so what's the point of you guys fighting it with me if you can't win. I prefer that you guys snitch on me so that you guys can get a low sentence and come out of prison to help continue to build what I have created"*

We were all sitting there with no words, Apache had tears rolling down his eyes, my heart was racing and my palms were sweaty. Ozzie just walked out of the room slamming the door as he walked out in disbelief.

KING BLOOD *"My brothers I know you don't want to do this. This*

THIS IS NOT USED

is the only thing I can do to save you guys. Believe me, this is for the best, this can not leave the room you are all sitting in. Them other niggas are just snitching on me and not saying the truth about themselves. They are not considered brothers in my eyes, so if you guys snitch on me and on them, then you will be helping your-selves and you will be destroying them for breaking the black rose and for trying to T.O.S. me, my brothers these are the last orders I will ever ask of you"

His voice just stopped, we sat there waiting to see if he would continue talking but the phone line was cut off. Neither one of us knew what to say or what to think. Apache finally spoke after a couple of minutes of silence

Apache " Ok My brothers, I know you don't like what you just heard but King Blood is our superior, in his own way this is his only way of fighting for us"

Apache continued speaking to us and the more he spoke the more sense it all made. Apache had spoken to us with the intention of calming us down . He explained that the brothers that were cooperating with the Feds were telling the whole truth about King Blood but they hid the true facts about their ac-tions within the nation. They made themselves out to be goody goodies. If we would obey Bloods orders, we would be destroy-ing their credibility as well as there 5kI.I letters. 5kI.I letters were letters that the United States Attorneys would write to the judges recommending leniency for cooperators. If they snitched and made the Prosecutors happy then they would win a Get out of Jail card. King Bloods plan was wonderful. I personally agreed with King Blood and King Apache. After several days of thinking it over, I receive a collect call from King Nel.

OPERATOR "You have a collect call from Nel , from a correctional facility, do you accept the call"

I accepted the call and waited a few seconds for Nel to begin speaking.

KING NEL "ADR My brother, how's everything out there?

I explained that things could be better and that it seemed as if everything is falling apart. I explained to Nel that the Nation seems to be splitting up and that every borough wants to claim superiority over the other.

KING NEL *"Forget that, I know Sangre spoke to you guys already, and shit looks like it's going to work, now we just have to make sure that some way somehow King Tone becomes Inka of New York.*

I was confused, why would we give King Tone, out of all people , so much power. This didn't make no sense to me. King Tone was a straight up Junky that none of us older brothers respected.

KING NEL *"He is one of Bloods enemies but Blood is sleeping him. He is one of those brothers that came out on T.V and nation wide stated that King Blood was a bad apple. Blood is not stupid , That was Tones way of double crossing Blood but Blood is playing the master of the game with him. Also if you remember the day Tone had asked us to go to his job in Manhattan. It was you , Ozzie, Kano, Little Pegs, Nellow and Tone. Tone had tried to use me and you so that we could kill Teardrop. Remember, he tried telling us that it was Bloods idea but we knew better. Blood didn't forget that either, this is all Bloods idea. Bloods been talking to Tone over the phone. He's going to give him a high ranking position and after that, he'll end up in here with the rest of us. Then the whole world is to going toWho the real bad apple is. This way the attentions away from all of us real niggas and the feds will be tracking that dumbass junkie."*

It was now making sense to me. I asked Nel what was it he needed from me and what should I tell the rest of the bros that were in the room with me the day Blood had spoken to us on the phone last week.

KING NEL *"Just tell them that they have to play their part if this is all to work out. By the way, keep away from the brothers in Bushwick. They are trifling brothers. I've heard through the grape vine , they are trying to start their own chapter. Gangsta Killa Queens. That's what they are trying to call themselves but they are made of mostly of snitches , like Apocalypse and Brain, they don't know that we have private investigators on their ass, they've been doing* *grimy shit, just keep away from them , that's all I'm telling you. ADR, and play your part.*That was all that was said, I didn't hear from King Nel for months after that.

19

Every Borough in N.Y. claimed to be superior to the other, the nation was in chaos everything was happening so fast. There were really no more Universals. King Tone became Inka 1st Supreme Crown of N.Y. State. He tried having Universals but only Bushwick and East New York would mainly show up , a couple of other brothers from other boroughs would show up as well but nothing close to the meetings we were having before. The Universals that King Tone were having, were so small that they decided to start having it in a small church. I just never understood why King Tone did it right across the street from a police precinct. Sunset Park was doing what Sunset Park did best. They banged on everybody and anybody. King Fonseca became 1st crown of Sunset , King Hitman became 2nd King Ozzie 3rd , of course I still held on to my position which was Fourth Crown and Little Peg was 5th Crown. King Tone being originally from East New York, he was trying to strip brothers from Sunset and Coney Island. This was easier said than done. Sunset Park was a tribe that was made up of 4 tribes into one. We had, Bay Ridge, Park Slope, Flatbush and Sunset Park.

We were one Tribe made up of 4 and just kept the name Sunset Park Tiger Tribe Division One. For as long as I can remember the other side of Brooklyn had always hated us but we truly didn't care. We were doing it up. I personally was stuck in the middle because I was hanging with my girl that lived in East New York and she lived very close to Kano , Tone, Nellow and the rest of Division 2. I had to make a choice either my girl or my brothers. It turned out that it wasn't as hard as I thought it would be. I chose my brothers. I began seeing one of the sisters from my tribe, Queen Angie. She lived with her mother Nelly on Bay Ridge Avenue. This sister was a freak in the bed. We fucked , all day and night, and for breakfast she had some of me. Sunset was ringing bells and everyone new it. The Feds were watching and The NYPD CAGE UNIT were watching as well. We Knew it and we just couldn't stop. King Tone was sending out hits but it was like sending a cat to a dog show. Whoever he sent would end up getting touched and being sent back to Tone. Division 2 had some real True Latin Kings that just got caught in the mix and sometimes they were just soldiers to Tone. He didn't love them or care about them, He had power now, he didn't give a shit about none of them. Many other Tribes felt as Sunset Park felt like for instance The Bronx. The Bronx was strong, they had no respect for Tone, yeah a few Kings from the Bronx were loyal to Tone but the real hard core Kings knew he was a fake . They read right through him. King Tone was seen as a hypocrite. He violated Latin Kings that were selling drugs but he sold drugs himself. He tried stripping real gully strong brothers from the family because other brothers looked up to them as leaders. He wanted all power and loyalty for himself. It turned out that even Latin Kings from his own Division broke away from him. Latin Kings from Bushwick that ran with Tone decided they were going to run their own show. They departed from King Tones grip and created an offset called The Gangsta Killa Queens. Everyone saw this as a sign of weakness from King Tone because we as Kings are suppose to claim Latin King Nation, nothing else, but Tone let it ride because he knew he wasn't going to win. He was weak, he knew it and the rest of the nation new it. Meanwhile over in Sunset a Latin King by the name of King Indio was released from Attica. Sunset was the first place for him to visit. Once in Sunset there was nowhere else he rather have been. He was extremely violent with his enemies but with us he was a teddy bear. Indio had a long scar on the right side of his face. Memories of O.B.C.C. in Rikers. He saw that Bloods were holding it down and they were trying to pressure the bros that were in there. Indio took it upon himself to put in work and mark them for life by cutting every Blood member he ran into. This earned him much time in the box as well as a cut on the face by one of his many victims. In Sunset he instantly made a name for himself. Drugs was his hustle but down low stick up was his specialty. He and I didn't really see to much eye to eye. Something about him made me feel as if he believed I was soft. He and King Little Pegs hit it off real quick. With Indio in Sunset Park It only made Division One that much more stronger. King Tone was not trying to have it. He began talking to Kings from Sunset Park secretly , offering them high ranking positions if they would side with him, this was his version of The Master of the Game. It *worked*, He made King Chino first crown for Sunset Park, King Shorty second crown for Sunset Park, King Ozzie was left at 3rd, I was left at 4TH and Little Pegs was 5th.

Now that he had Chino and Shorty at the two top positions for Sunset park, he would use them to try and set up Ozzie, Little Pegs and Myself. He began talking negative about King Blood, saying that King Blood used us and he was not worth being Godfather of this nation. He began taping a documentary called Latin Kings with HBO. This was exactly what King Blood had hoped for. Many old timers that were locked up were not liking the fact that King Tone was putting all our Kings affairs out in public. They began writing letters to the outside world demanding that King Tone be dealt with accordingly. King Tone was well aware of this, therefore he began wearing a bullet proof vest and walked with 2 to 4 Kings along side of him at all times. King Bloods plan was working better than what he had expected. The Feds were on Tones ass like fly on shit. There was nothing Tone could have done about it. Tone sent King Jayrock to T.O.S King Ozzie and cut off the Tattoo Ozzie had on his left forearm. July 5th 1995, King Ozzie is sitting on one of the benches in Sunset Park with one of his girlfriends who many believed was a police officer herself. While sitting on the bench having their conversation, she warned him about a suspicious young Hispanic creeping behind him. Ozzie feeling comfortable, didn't put much mind to it. The mysterious looking individual was King Jayrock in disguise. He reached out behind Ozzie's back, held down Ozzie's arm and took 3 full swings at it, cutting his arm deeply and destroying the tattoo. Jayrocks mission failed. He was suppose to kill him but before he can do anymore damage King Ozzie quickly pulled out a nickel plated 45 semi-automatic and aimed it right at King Jayrocks head.

Ozzie *"O.K. if you answer my questions truthfully I might not shoot you."*

King Jayrock was practically shitting in his pants, knowing that if he runs he won't make it away.

Ozzie *"Ok, you think I'm playing"* (Ozzie, hitting him over the head, blood cushing from the top of his right eye made by the blunt impact of the butt of the semiautomatic) **Jayrock** *"Ok, ok, it was Tone, he sent me, he gave me a direct order!*

King Ozzie pistol whipped him once again sending him back to Tone bloody. Ozzie called me and decided he wanted to discuss with me about King Bloods plan. He was on board.

Meanwhile back at the M.C.C, Latin Kings were confused about who to trust who and not to trust. Every day a member of The Latin Kings was calling their attorneys trying to make deals with the United States Attorneys Office. King Teardrop himself offered to testify against members of the Latin Kings but his offer was immediately shut down by the United States

Office. Other Members were transferred over to the second floor of the Metropalitan Correctional Center where they signed on to the Wit-sec Unit(Witness protection Unit). On September 1995, the Feds hit us again, this time Locking up King Chino, King Greeneyes, King Mousey, King Tito, King Culebra. Luckily for myself I wasn't home that day, because they went to my house looking for me. I called King Ozzie, I told him I would be in Brooklyn 42nd Street in Sunset I needed his help to try and get away, maybe go to N.J. He was no where to be found. That same night I walked over to 37th street and fourth looking to see if I see him working there but as I am leaving Queen Darlas house, the Gang Unit was there. It was that fucking prick Louis Lally and Brian Savelli. The same cops we would call Starsky and Hutch. They had me surrounded, there was no place I could go. I was cuffed and read my rights. I went directly to the Metropolitan Correctional Center. I was indicted for the Murder of Victor Lirschman and the attempted murder of King Mousey. I wasn't really stressed out, actually I felt relieved because I was honestly getting tired of running. I needed to just get the shit over with already. There I was sent to the hole at 9 South where I was only let out one hour a day for rec. On my recreation time I saw a few of the brothers but I remembered everything that King Blood had said to us that day in the room. My worst enemies were all around me. I just didn't know who was who.

King Epic *"Yo, Macho, Amor De Rey, what's really good. When did they bag you?"*

Myself *"Last night, I'll be aight!"*

King Epic *"I heard Queen Angie is going to have your baby!"*

Myself *"Nah, I think you heard wrong. A.D.R!"*

That was as far as the conversation got because I knew he was one of the ones that tried getting King Blood T.O.S. I noticed a few other brothers where there but they were keeping to themselves. Two days later I was sent to Ottisville Facility. There I was placed in population and I saw all the brothers. King Kano, King Nellow, King Nel, King Apollo, King Chino and a few other brothers. While there I was asked by King Kano to be a look out while they gave King Chino a physical out the family. Normally you get killed if you try to leave but he was shown love because he had enough years in the nation, so they just gave him his 5 minute physical and he was no longer a King. I was more than sure that Chino was up to no good. He was always acting weird as if he had something to hide. I also noticed that there were inmates in there that had gotten 15 to even 20 years for just a gun possession but Chino had gotten only 10 years for conspiracy to murder. If no one said anything about this it's cause they had no proof. But I am more than sure he had to have done some kind of talking or some kind of deal. Many believed that he was given the opportunity to collaborate other cooperators information. Since he did this, he probably received some kind of leniency for his information. My mind began working hard. Remembering King Bloods words. I called my attorney and asked for him to set up a meeting with the US Attorneys office. I then went to the yard and looked for King Nel.

Myself *"Nel, what's up , are you doing your thing as Blood ordered us to or what?"*

NEL *"Yeah man, I am but we can't be talking about this shit. You do what you gotta do and remember that most of these brothers are not really our brothers, they tried killing Blood up in MCC. Just do what you gotta do and The Master Of The Game should work just fine"*

Myself *"I don't feel right about this shit, no one is going to understand or believe none of this shit. How long do you think I'll be able to stay here in population before these niggas catch on?"*

Nel *"I don't know , but I'm suppose to testify against Blood soon, so I'll be back at MCC in a few wks, shit, I don't feel right about this either but Blood is* *right, this is his way of saving us niggas that really put in work for him. The hell with the rest of them niggas that shitted on him. Don't you notice some of these niggas in the yard with us are trying to run under Chicago. After all Bloods done for us now they are going to shit on his name. Blood was right to do what he's doing. Blood Line forever baby!*

Myself *"Aight then, I'll do my thing but never will anybody believe Blood ordered us to do this shit."*

20

Here I am in my cell, and I'm thinking to myself, where are all those brothers out there in the world that had said they loved me. Where are all those people that screamed out the words Amor De Rey. I promised myself that if and when I get out of this hell hole I was not going back to the streets , there was no way I was going to end up here again. I learned a lot while in prison. The people that promised you to be there for you aren't there. My girlfriend whom I was engaged to, where was she. I would call the house collect and she would not accept it. I would write to her everyday and if I ever got a letter from her it was a miracle. I would call my lawyers office and ask if he can put me on a 3-way so that I can speak to my fiancé. The phone would ring,

Fiancé *"Hello?"*

Myself *"What's up ma, it's me, why haven't you written to me, I miss you so much, why don't you accept my collect calls?"*

Fiancé *"Ah, How were you just able to call me, ah, umm, I cant speak right now, I'm doing something for work"*

Mans voice in Background *"Come on baby, hang up the phone, I need some of that!"*

Myself *"Who the fuck was that, what the fuck is going on here , didn't you say you love me, didn't you promise me that you would be there for me, damn it's only been a short time I've been here!"*

Fiancé *"Ah, I'm sorry, the phone is messed up, call me some other time"*

I couldn't believe my fucking ears, here I was in a 9 by 10 fucking cell going crazy, wanting to die cause I miss my freedom, my family, my fiancé, my life, and this bitch is fucking the next man. I cried myself to sleep for months. I had to be strong if not, I was going to end up dead. I began thinking of what King Blood had told us in that room that day. I realized I still had a chance to be free. Ok maybe I'd do a couple of years but 3 or 4 was way better than 25 to life. Several days later I was in the United States Attorneys office, telling them all they wanted to hear. They said they won't need me to testify, they were only using my information to verify someone else's story. I was promised a 5kI.I letter for my cooperation. Knowing that King Blood had ordered me to do this, it didn't make any difference, I felt like an ass doing it but at least there was a light at the end of the tunnel for me, which is more than what I can say for King Bloods betrayers. Word was that King Tone was all over the news, he was in Magazines and even on HBO. The Kings in Sunset Park were going at it with King Tone and the rest of his followers. Tone wasn't just getting high on drugs, now he was high on the power that he was holding. This was something I knew would be his downfall. King Blood had once told me that Power is a very dangerous enemy, it clouds your mind, tricks you into believing you are something that you really aren't. Making Power one of the most dangerous enemies of all. I realize that I was better off being were I was so that I can start making myself strong both mentally and physically. I worked out, I read books and I kept away from all the negative people around me, I kept mostly to myself. Oct 2 1996, I am up early, playing pool at the MCC, and to my surprise, I see King Chucky. He was a Latin King brother I had bumped into at Otisville Correctional Facility. He was doing a bid of 5 years. He was telling me all the gossip about the other brothers. He had told me how King Fonseca had gotten stabbed by King Assassin. He had also told me how King Chino had suspiciously come back to the family again, he believed there was more to it but wasn't really sure. The most interesting thing that caught my attention was about King Ozzie. He stated Ozzie was in 7 North in MCC just 2 floors below me. I was wondering if he followed King Bloods order or not. Last I heard was that he was in Putnam Correctional Facility with King Tee and King Shorty holding it down. He had gotten poked up on his left side of his ribs right below his armpit. I was also told that when he was shipped to Valhalla Westchester Facility, he had run into King Teardrop. Teardrop believed that Ozzie was part of the meeting that was held in King Tone's old job. Teardrop didn't want to believe anything Ozzie had to say, word through the grapevine was that Ozzie and Teardrop fought for about 30 minutes in the yard without the C.O's stopping. Rumor was that the C.O's themselves placed bets on who would win. I would have probably place my money on my old Third Crown. Eventually I saw Ozzie at the MCC, actually we became cellmates.

Myself *"My bro, what's up, why you so down?"*

Ozzie *"It's sad on how this whole shit turned out man, I never in my wildest dreams would have believed that I would be in the predicament I'm in right now"*

Myself *"I feel you big bro but just hold your head, we'll be aight!"*

Ozzie *"Damn son, why would these niggas shit on Blood the way they did? And why the hell niggas is trying to act like they gully when I know half of these niggas out there in streets with Tone is ass"*

Myself *"I don't know my bro but I'm leaving it alone, when I'm out of here, I aint going back.*

Ozzie *"Nah, fuck that, Imma be out there, let them niggas try and bring it, Imma real King and real Niggas do real things.*

Myself *"Yeah you never change always a 3rd crown huh?"*

A year later Ozzie was send to Ottisville. It turned out that he had obeyed King Blood's orders sooner than what we all had thought. Hey I don't knock him. Anyone that knew the truth would feel the same way I did.

21

Today's the big day, I couldn't sleep all night last night. Tossing and turning and praying for the best preparing for the worst. I woke up early, got my breakfast and read the Daily news that the OIC (officer in charge) had lend me. I couldn't believe my eyes. King Tone was indicted and arrested by the FBI yesterday on drug charges. Out of all things drug charges. I recall King Tone violating many of my brothers from Sunset Park because they sold drugs. I recall King Tone coming out on TV talking about how positive he is running the Nation. Well we all knew better and I guess King Bloods plans turned out just as he had suspected. How was he able to look into the future and see all of this happen I don't know but this was his best Master Of The Game ever.

King Blood had gotten sentenced to life in prison without the possibility of parole. During the time that King Nel was testifying against King Blood, King Blood sneakily gave King Nel a small wink as if saying, It's all working out as I planned. The Jury chairman said the word guilty 21 times. He was to remain in solitary confinement for the remainder of his life. King Blood was ordered to completely have no communication with anyone, including his friends and including non immediate family members. This was done so that he would not be able to send out hits from inside as he was found guilty of already. This was to be the last that the entire Almighty Latin King Nation was to hear from him personally. As I sat on my bed I realized how much in danger I was going to be in if and when I get out of this hellhole. No one was ever going to believe what really happened. I realized that no matter what, I was going to have to live with the fact that someway somehow someone was going to try and kill me. It will probably be someone who was going to try and make a name for themselves. The Latin Kings were no longer the same. There was no togetherness, no love, just hunger for power and control. This gave every other organization the opportunity to build and become strong. The Latin Kings were now seen as a weak gang that was not united. Latin Kings from Bushwick in Brooklyn were trying to claim superiority over the rest of N.Y. They would talk negative about the Bronx and Manhattan claiming that they were soft and weak. Till this day there is no unity and instead of fighting the oppression as they were originally created for, they were now fighting each other but come to think of it. They've always done this and I was not planning to be part of it again. Dead or alive, I'm leaving it alone. My parents and my blood brothers are the only ones there for me. Thinking about this, I decided to write to my mother to thank her for being there for me when no one else is.

I had to put that to the side, in just a few hours I was going to court.

December19, 1998—9:00am, I am standing at the defendants table waiting for my sentence. Looking back I could see my mother and father sitting there praying to god to forgive me for all my sins. My hands couldn't stop shaking, I was nervous and my heart was beating a hundred miles an hour. My palms were so sweaty that the sweat was dripping down my fingertips. Judgement day was in process. Honorable Judge Larry McGuiness was my sentencing Judge.

Judge "*After reading this 5k1.1 letter and some considerable thought, I must agree with the United States attorney with their recommendation of time served plus 5 years probation.*

I couldn't believe my ears, tears rolling down my eyes, that second chance in life was now mine. I promised the world that I will do the best I can to never go back to the streets. From this day forward I will do the best I can not to ever end up here again. For the first time I was being held and hugged by both my parents. For all those years I wished my father was there, that was the past. My dad was here for me now and he and I have our whole future ahead of us to make up for our past mistakes. My mother held me with all her might thanking god for answering her prayers. For all that's ever happened in the past with my mother and I, I forgave her right there and then. This was going to be my new beginning.

My brothers just smiled and winked at me, knowing his big brother was coming back home now. No more days for me that felt like months and no more months for me that felt like years. I was a free man. King Blood was right, everything worked out exactly as he had planned. All those that tried to go against the grain, ended up dead or behind bars for a very long time. All of those brothers and sisters that double crossed him were now being double crossed by The King Of all Kings in ways they would have never imagined. I had recalled how on March 30th 1995 he had written his last words. There are so many hidden messages in it and those brothers that were in that room with us that day , they know what he was really saying in that manifesto. This manifesto will be the only thing I will take with me in my new life, everything else is staying behind those bars.

22

My family was still living in the hood, Sunset Park. I decided to live in my mother's house until I got myself on my feet and got myself someplace to live. Everyone already knew I was out of jail before I even got to the hood. Many of my old childhood friends were happy to see me. Of course one of the first things I did was to get me some Punani. I met up with an old friend Lena she showed me one hell of a good time. First place she took me to was to the Golden Gate Hotel. This is where she performed the most wonderful crazy oral sex I ever had. This girl was the bomb diggity. I could honestly say she gave me one hell of a welcome home gift. It was a matter of days before The Almighty Latin King Nation realized I was back home. Did they know what happened, I wasn't sure but I knew I'd fine out soon enough. King Skiddy came to see me with a few other bros. He was supposedly the son to the nation. He told everyone that he was crowned by King Blood but I didn't believe that at all. Everyone else did so I just let it ride. It didn't really mean much to me anyway since I was done with all this nonsense.

King Skiddy *"A.D.R my brother, welcome home. How does it feel to be home?"*

Myself *"It feels good, I'm planning on just doing what I have to do to stay out of jail. No more streets for me, you can tell the Nation that I'm done with it."*

King Skiddy *" Well you know there was a rumor that you snitched right, so I think that your best bet is come back and clear your name, while you're at it, help us get it back to where it once was"*

Myself *"Nah pah, I'm not going that route, I did my time, I shed my blood* *for this nation and there are things that went on that none of you guys would be able to understand, so before niggas start talking shit, Imma just leave it alone and get on with my life."*

King Skiddy *" Look Macho, your name rings bells, whether negative or positive, you're the talk of the town right now, you got 500 Kings that want to kill you on one side and then you got 500 Kings that want you as their leader on the other, you got to deal with it one way or the other"*

Myself *" Look my bro, tell Dave, Noel, Hector Torres and the rest of the Brothers. They wanna see me and do me dirty, that's on them but , I'm a Lion , retired from this Nation or not, I'm still a Lion. Just let me be!*

King Skiddy *"Aight then my brother, if that's how you want it then so be it, you're on your own. ADR"*

Myself *"Yeah ok, whatever!"*

I had gotten the impression that this was not going to be the last I heard from King Skiddy. I have always had my doubts about him. He was one of those brothers that had been around for many years. He's been through everything and anything and still he had managed to keep himself out of prison. This I found interesting. He was well known throughout the entire state of N.Y. This Brother was one of those that would double cross even his own mother if he had to. I was going to have to keep 2 extra set of eyes behind my head just to be on the safe side.

I found myself a job on Downtown Fulton at an electrical appliance store. Things were looking up for me, I had myself a wifey, I got myself an apartment and my probation officer was off my back as long as I was doing what I had to do to better myself. The Almighty Latin King Nation was now a thing of the past.

I was working out at 5th avenue Gym so that I can keep in shape. Once in a blue moon I would run into a Latin King here or there, they would always say the same thing.

King Capone " *Amor De Rey, Macho, when are you coming back to hold us down, we need you?"*

Myself *"Nah, it aint for me no more, I'll keep it in my mind and heart, I'll live as a King my way, the right way!"*

King Capone *"You know they tried to say you snitched right? Them niggas from 180! They've been plotting on you."*

Myself *"Yeah, aight let them come see me if they want, either way , I ain't going back , they are all about nothing anyway, who they think I am , Relic?"*

King Capone *"True, true, just don't let them niggas know I put you on to what they are saying ok, see you around the hood, ADR*

23

Ladies and Gentleman this is Lisa Lolita of Street warrior at 67.4fm, as I was telling the story of a gang member named Macho, where was I? Oh yeah, OK, Macho had refused to go back out to the streets and go back to his old ways. Listeners let me tell you, this was easier said than done. Macho never denied being a Latin King but all he wanted was a second chance in life. He had explained to his superiors that he was walking a different walk now, the walk of life. They refused to let Macho live his life. They felt they needed him to come back because if he did then many of Machos followers would come back with him. "No means no and if you can't respect that then come and get me " Ladies and gentle men it's sad to say that Macho is no longer with us, he is now in heaven. He was killed 4 weeks ago by members of the Almighty Latin King Nation. He refused to go back to the streets. They were calling but this time he learned his lesson, but as many young gang members from the early 80's up to the early nineties, there was no way out. Ladies and gentlemen this is Lisa Lolita of street warriors saying goodbye and goodnight, next week I will be taking calls on this story and we will be talking to gang members that knew King Macho.

Good afternoon Ladies and Gentlemen this is Lisa Lolita with Street Warriors at 67.4fm. Just last week I told you a story about a Latin King Member who went by the name of King Macho. He grew up in Sunset Park a good kid but ended up taking the wrong path. He went to prison for acts he committed while being a member of the Latin Kings and after 3 and a half years he was released. He refused to go back to the streets and vowed to take advantage of the second chance he got in life. I personally got to meet him and he seemed to be on the up and up. Just 5 weeks ago he was killed. It is being assumed that members of the Latin Kings killed him, some say because he refused to go back to the street life, others say he was killed because he cooperated with the government. I am now taking calls from my listeners and letting you all hear what they feel about King Macho's situation.

Lisa Lolita "King Score, what are your thoughts about what has happened and how can we help stop what seems to be a issue here in our streets of NY.

King Score " I personally knew King Macho, he was loved by few and hated by many, I had much respect for this brother and my prayers are with him"

Lisa Lolita " How we as members of the community can help young kids from the streets, how can we help them avoid being in a position and predicament that King Macho was in?"

King Score " Look man, I just had and still have much love for the bro, that's all I have to say!"

Lisa Lolita " Ok then, on with our next caller, King Tiny from Shaou-lin. Your comment about last weeks Street Warriors story"

King Tiny "Well, the word on the street was that he snitched but if he was a snitch then he had me fooled cause he was one of the realest Kings I've ever met, He was a good brother."

Lisa Lolita "Now we have King Ducky from Bushwick Brooklyn, your comments sir"

King Ducky "Man the hell with that dude, why you wasting your time on him for, he was a snitch"

Lisa Lolita *"Did you personally know him?*

King Ducky *"Nah I didn't chill with the dude but I heard he was no good so (Beeeeeeep Beeeep Beeeep) that's what I have to say.*

Lisa Lolita *" Oh ok, hold on Ducky, I have someone that has something to say in reference to your comment. Ok, Apache you're on the air"*

King Apache *" Yeah, cats like King Ducky didn't really get along with King Macho cause Macho was to serious for them, Macho was not the type to take an iron and burn someone's Tattoo off just to prove a point , unlike certain lucky thugs that wanna press their luck"*

Lisa Lolita " Sorry folks we lost King Apache, well *we have a Sgt. Louis Savelli from the NYPD CAGE UNIT*

SGT. Savelli *" I recall locking this kid up outside of a club on 36th and Fourth after he was on the run for about 5 months. Once the cuffs were on I could see a sense of relief , as if he was saying to himself "Thank God this is over" While we were questioning him , I recall his last words to me were, Once this is all over, I'm gonna start my life over fresh , no matter how long I stay in jail, once out , I'm going to do the right thing. I honestly believed him. I'ts a shame he never got the chance.*

Lisa Lolita *"Oh ok , King Apache is back on the line, sorry there, we had lost you for a minute. Did you personally know King Macho? And if you did, what type of person was he?"*

King Apache *"Ah man, he was a real stand up character, never took no (Beeeep) from anybody, always stood up for those chosen few that he had respect and love for"*

Lisa Lolita *"Listeners, we have a call from someone at Rikers Island calling, Bloody Shawn"*

Bloody Shawn *"Yeah, I remember the man he was a real mellow kinda man, He was about the only Puerto Rican that try to lock horns with us here at this house I'm at right now, every other King that was in our house, we ran out but not King Macho, there was much respect for the kid, ya feel me, by the way, 031 to all my dogs , where ya at!"*

Lisa Lolita *"Ok, we have 2 more callers and then we are going to have to go to a commercial break, Detective Camello you're on the air"*

Detective Camello *"Yeah, I had arrested the subject once and he struck me to be a very intelligent individual, I just can't comprehend why is it that these guys out there can take hours everyday studying gang mumbo jumbo, but they refuse to study in school, or go to college. This Macho obviously made a few mistakes but he nor anyone else should ever pay with their lives. It's a shame."*

Lisa Lolita *"Ok, We have one more call to take then we are going to take a break for just a few minutes, next caller is Little Macho from Brooklyn"*

Little Macho *"Where's my daddy?*

Lisa Lolita *"Wait, how old are you, are you related to the Macho we are speaking about?"*

Little Macho *"I love you daddy, please come back home."*

Female voice in background *"Hey, come here, who you on the phone with, hang up that phone now Macho"*

Little Macho *"Tell my daddy I love him, gotta go, bye"*

Coming Soon

LITTLE MACHOS REVENGE
by Brandon Cory